THE NUT FILE

THE NUT FILE

John Skoyles

QUALE PRESS

Several of these pieces have appeared in *The American Poetry Review*, *The Boston Globe*, *The Christian Science Monitor*, *Freshwater Review* and *Ibbetson Street*, in slightly different form.

ISBN: 978-1-935835-21-9 trade paperback edition

LCCN: 2017931289

Quale Press
www.quale.com

For Tony Hoagland

Author's Note

When I was in college, I worked for the Associated Press at 50 Rockefeller Center in New York City. I sorted mail, typed and filed documents. One day, I found a fat manila folder labeled, NUT FILE. A reporter told me it was a collection of memos, articles and letters—most of them bizarre, others well-meaning, a few of them touching, some ridiculously misguided—that the newsmen had gathered for their entertainment. On a slow news day, one of the writers would grab the folder and amuse his colleagues by reading aloud from it.

This book is my own nut file, an anthology of many voices: friends, relatives, strangers, reporters, as well as that of the author. Some stories and anecdotes come directly from literary works by Jimmy Cannon, Truman Capote, Harold Clurman, Isaac Dinesan, Jim Harrison, Georges Perec and Mary Heaton Vorse, among others.

I stick out my tongue, he reaches into his pocket, pulls out a jackknife, opens it, and brings the blade close to my face. He says, "Now we'll cut off his tonue." But he does not cut off my tongue, he only carves the letter *g* from that word.

We swam in the North River, off the docks. The little guy was a stranger, a Polish kid, and he was very brave. He went off the roof of the pier in a swan dive. We waited for him to come up but he didn't. We dressed and stood around while the cops dragged the waters with hooks and his mother stood there, screaming. They located him after a while and the hooks pulled him up. His head was jammed into a milk can which must have been standing on the river floor. The mother stopped screeching and started to turn down the dock, her apron strings streaming out behind her. She seemed blinded by her grief because when she came to the police cord, she didn't falter. It tripped her and she fell into the river. A cop dove in and he had to punch her senseless before he could get her back to the wooden ladder of the dock. They forgot about the dead boy with his head in the milk can and worked on his unconscious mother.

On April 29, 2000, *The New York Times* obituary page noted the deaths of two men: Gregory Gillespie, "An Unflinching Painter"; and Toon Hermans, "Practitioner of the Gentle Art of Fun Onstage." Gillespie's photo was taken beside a somber self-portrait. The painter is described as having "an unflinching scrutiny that gave his work a disturbing edge. He regularly turned this scrutiny on himself." The obituary writer said his self-portraits "recorded his changing appearance and shifting moods and always pivoted on his intense blue eyes, which suggested that a profound secret might be revealed if one stared hard enough." Gillespie's death was a suicide.

Toon Hermans, "a beloved Dutch stage performer," often had audiences "crying with laughter." Among his songs was one about a little balloon and another describing a man desperately searching for his clown nose to wear to a party. Toon's most famous tragic-comic act was "the sketch of the magician who finds his beloved dove is dead." "I will never take leave," he told Amsterdam's *De Telegraaf* newspaper on his eightieth birthday. "At a certain point, life will do it for me." He died of a heart attack.

I came home from school one day and told my Italian grandfather that we learned that Jesus performed miracles. He asked me to explain. I said that Jesus went to a wedding and changed water into wine. My grandfather thought for a moment and said, "It seems to me this miracle is worth nothing more than the price of a bottle of wine."

Found in my aunt's apartment after her death:

> A manila envelope containing a swizzle stick from P. J. Clarke's.
>
> Matchbooks from Jack Dempsey's and Il Vagabondo (a restaurant whose tables bordered a bocce court).
>
> Cards from funeral masses for relatives, and the obituary of her father—a roofer who "fell six

stories from the National Sugar Refinery in New Jersey, landed on a railroad car filled with pig iron and was killed."

A photo of prizefighter Tony Canzoneri, taken at the Beverly Farm resort in the Catskills, where she vacationed each summer for a week. Tony's thick arms are folded across his knit shirt, his head tossed back in laughter, giving even more prominence to his well-pummeled nose. Clipped to the picture is a newspaper column entitled, "Building a Universe on the Basis of a Man's Slim Remark," in which the writer recounts falling for men who allured her with words. As far as we knew, my prim aunt had no lover in her life but it seems she had a crush on the holder of three world boxing titles.

Her fortune-teller's deck. Passion was the subject of every forecast. The image of a life preserver signaled a voyage to or from romance. The bright engagement ring meant happiness. The tea set, gossip. She used to set up a folding table in her living room and predict the futures of our neighbors. As she shuffled the deck, she insisted it had no bearing on the truth. But if she turned the image of the pierced heart, she winced visibly, unable to stop herself from saying, "I hate to see that card!" and shaking her visitor to the core.

A postcard I sent her from Dallas, where I had moved for my first real job. My salary made me feel so flush that on Valentine's Day I sent bouquets to her and my mother. My mother loved the surprise, but the florist phoned me, troubled, as my aunt refused to open her door. The more the delivery boy pleaded, the more certain she felt his words were a criminal's ruse to enter her apartment. The florist reported her saying, "No one's sending me any flowers."

I sent them again, this time for her funeral, when they could not be refused.

During his quest for spiritual enlightenment, my friend apprenticed himself to a *roshi*, a Zen Buddhist master, who could hardly speak English. For lunch, he offered my friend a "penis butter and jelly sandwich," and apologized for meeting him early one morning still wearing his "vaginas."

My father had no friends. He said, "As long as I have a buck in my pocket, I don't need a friend."

If you have a brother and he loves cheese, that's physics. If you have a brother and *therefore* he loves cheese, that's metaphysics. If you *don't* have a brother and he loves cheese, that's pataphysics.

My aunt asked what I liked about kindergarten. I said nap time because that's when we lie on our mats and look up girls' dresses. My aunt said that if I did that, God would blow a piece of dust into my eye.

Fifty years later, fifty years of that same activity in different contexts and afflicted with corneal erosion, I'm sure he did.

The surgeon, a professor at a medical school, was reading applications for admission. "My first question when reviewing candidates," he said, "is whether they will kill somebody."

The poet, a professor at a university, was reading applications to the MFA Program in poetry. "My first question when reviewing candidates," he said, "is whether they will kill themselves."

Brain-damaged Brian Denner was never a figure of fun in our neighborhood of unusually cruel children. He sat in a rusty chair on his stoop, rubbing the bridge of his long nose. We always waved and he sometimes waved back. We tried to engage him in conversation, but his words were confused. When he returned from family vacations and we asked how it went, he always answered, "Same but different." He said this about holidays, birthdays and weddings. As a child, I found it paradoxical. As an adult, perfect sense.

Our Lady's is a nice place except for the very infirm. I'm sure it is hard for Aunt Grace to see herself living among people so disabled. A nurse said they are referred to as the Os and the Qs depending on how their mouths look and the position of their tongues.

Everything is the same and everything is different.

The English Department bulletin board is known as the Wall of Fame. It contains poems, articles and stories published by faculty members. If your name doesn't appear, you seem lazy and unproductive. After a long dry spell, Mary Yindell tacked up a story about herself from her local paper. It reported that she was "fortunate to have just learned the secret to removing Christmas tree sap from animal fur when her cat, Jonathan Livingston Seagull, got his head stuck to his chest at 2:30 in the morning." The photo shows Mary holding the cat by the neck and applying Skippy peanut butter with a stick.

Probably the first French poet to use the word *clitoris* in a poem, Jules Laforgue was shy of its proprietress out of verse…

I was reading through the stuffs today. Poetry has become a real part of me now. I am sure you know, but our whole class really did learn and appreciated from you. If not yet poets, you have given the inspiration to yearn to become one.

Our well-loved and distinguished colleague retired after fifty years of teaching Victorian Literature. A slight and gentle soul, always in a blue suit and solid tie, he had become almost deaf and was forced into emeritus status. We wondered what would happen to him, as he was born to the lectern. Watching him walk to class, shrinking from the crowd, head down, dodging anyone who knew him, I was reminded of seeing baseball great Willie Mays outside the Polo Grounds, uncomfortable in a shirt and tie. In the stadium, he was at ease, born to roam a field of grass with a piece of cowhide fitted to his hand. In the same way, our colleague seemed alive only in the lecture hall.

8

He lived alone, and had no relatives; the students were his family and the college his home. After his farewell party, it was agreed that each of us would call him once a week to check on his well-being. The department secretary drew up a chart. In the beginning, I dreaded the calls, as they involved shouting into the receiver with considerable exertion and constant misunderstanding. But what he said was always inviting and often astounding: he had just added a small auditorium to his already enormous mansion; covered the cage of his canary, a waterslager that sang like a falling stream. He had spent the morning gathering Asiatic lilies in his acre of garden, in the company of his housekeeper, a beautiful woman named Delight. He was finishing a rare burgundy with a visitor, a chess grandmaster he had almost defeated. My colleagues and I compared notes, amazed and even envious.

My Uncle Fred told my female cousin to say, whenever she was approached by a lascivious male, "How naïve you are!" He told me to answer, whenever I was approached by the same, "I don't swing that way, Jack." He told us both to request, whenever we were in a piano bar, "Anything by Gershwin."

I'm sure it's nothing.

Our retired Victorian specialist told our department chair that he had just climbed down from an eleven foot ladder, clearing oak leaves from his copper gutters, where he found a martini glass that someone had flung skyward at one of his summer extravaganzas.

A party has a beginning, a middle and an end, but not necessarily in that order.

My friend, a tree surgeon, lived in a house so big you didn't notice the two magnolias in the living room. He bought a watch dog, a Rottweiler, trained to check every door for intruders, but Willow became neurotic because her job never ended—there were ninety-five doors. It was like washing the windows of the U.N. building—when finished, time to start over. The dog needed something else to do and bit the electrician and the plumber. On walks, it lunged at the ankles of cyclists. My friend's wife feared being sued and wanted to get rid of Willow. They fought and nearly divorced. One day his wife called me, relieved, their debate over. They were about to split up, and when my friend left for work that morning, she was dialing a lawyer. She told me, breathlessly and tearfully, that God had intervened. I asked how, and she said that Willow had bitten the lip of the landscaper's young son, tearing it to his cheek. At that, even my friend agreed the dog had to go and the marriage was saved. His wife said, "God writes straight with crooked lines."

If God performs an Act of God and then regrets it, does He doubt He is God? And if God doubts Himself, is He an agnostic?

Given his personality, it was inevitable that James Purdy would be isolated from the literary mainstream. When you write a long, strange book, and call it *The House of the Solitary Maggot*, you can't expect a large audience.

10

A career has a beginning, a middle and an end, but not necessarily in that order.

I told her that I once had a Siamese cat named Toma. She lived to be twelve, and we traveled everywhere together. All over the world. And when she died I never had the heart to get another.

"Then maybe you'll understand this," she said, leading me over to the deep-freeze, and opening it. Inside was nothing but cats—dozens of them. "All my old friends. Gone to rest. It's just that I couldn't bear to lose them. *Completely*." She laughed, and said, "I guess you think I'm a bit dotty."

Middleweight Marvin Hagler fought Kevin Finnegan from England in a fight billed as Finnegan's Wake.

Dear John,

I just wanted to let you know that my Guggenheim application was not approved. I really appreciate your help, though. I'll probably apply in a few more years, when I have some new work published. Meanwhile, Caitlin and I are going to Italy for the month of April.

For some reason a copy of your book of essays appeared in our bathroom recently and I've been enjoying them very much.

Thanks,
William

The world is in flames and *The New Yorker* has a story containing this sentence, "The oysters in Nova Scotia are incomparable."

Just a hamburger and a cup of coffee, Ma'am. Thank you.

Pete Best was fired as the drummer of the Beatles and replaced by Ringo Starr. Years later, he released his own LP, *Best of the Beatles*.

Middleweight Champion Marvin Hagler easily defeated Venezuelan Fulgencio Obelmejias. There was not much interest in a rematch, but opponents for the powerful Hagler were hard to find, so the promoters tried to trick fight fans by changing the challenger's name to Fully Obel.

I took a job directing a non-profit arts organization that was near bankruptcy. The previous director had tried to use the interest from the endowment of $225,000 to pay the mortgage of $750,000. The board of trustees ordered me to meet with Stanley Kunitz, one of the organization's founders, as he had made great gains in the stock market.

I sipped martinis with Stanley on his porch, while he squinted at *The Wall Street Journal* which he kept folding into smaller and smaller squares, reading charts. I held a pen and legal pad. Stanley explained that he would select a list of the best mutual funds as rated by Morningstar. He explained the guide gave the best funds a grade of 1 and the worst a 5. He mixed another round of martinis, and went back to scrutinizing the figures. He read out various funds—Fidelity, Vanguard, T. Rowe Price and, after a third martini, I had a long list which he asked me to recite so he could choose a range for our portfolio. Another martini. We were both drunk but we had the list. Stanley stared into his garden, then picked up the paper again, brought it almost to his nose, and said, "I thought something was wrong. The highest rating is 5, and the lowest 1. Come back tomorrow!"

Francis "Iron Man" Joseph, a Provincetown native known for many years as the town drunk, died of cancer in his trailer home in North Truro.

Despite his severe alcoholism, which landed him in jail every winter for his own safekeeping, Mr. Joseph will always be remembered for clambering out of his disease by strength of will and character, sobering up and staying sober.

He got his personal nickname "Iron Man" for his incredible physical strength.

He never learned to read, but could quote the works of Ben Franklin, Robert Frost and Oliver Wendell Holmes. He memorized passages as they were read to him by fellow inmates at the county farm, also known as the Barnstable House of Correction, during the many cold winter months he spent there.

Before he stopped drinking, he used to be taken into custody frequently by the Provincetown police as an incapacitated person. Come winter, it was his custom to break a window so he could be sent to the farm where he would be warm and well fed.

Mr. Joseph once smashed a storefront window at Bryant's Market where liquor bottles were displayed. When the police arrested him with one of the bottles in his hands, he told them, "You can't prove anything. I was wearing gloves!"

He became legendary as the man who bent the inch-thick bars in the jail cell door. The Chief of Police, James

Meads, said, "He actually bent them. He was strong as an ox."

He couldn't read, but he always walked around with a newspaper.

He was sixty-six years old.

Jean said, "What do you think of friends?" I was surprised, but babbled on about how they might be the most important people in one's life, not the same as lovers, of course, but desperately needed, a second family, essential…

Lighting a cigarette, she said, "Yes, I must give them up." And it became clear she had meant the word *cigarettes* or *smokes* when she said *friends*. And I remembered something: years back, a mutual friend had described cigarettes as "twenty little friends in a pack—twenty friends always available…" I thought: Could there be a memory behind the choice of every mistaken word?

Sumgai is a word used among fountain pen enthusiasts. You go to a yard sale which has just opened and expect they might have a whole load of nice pens, pen parts, etc., and then you ask the folks there whether they have any. They reply, "Some guy bought all of them this morning."

Theaters used to show newsreels when I was a kid, and one contained clips of Floyd Patterson's heavyweight championship fights with Ingemar Johansson, a Swedish boxer. Johansson lifted his left fist toward the camera and said, "Toon-der!" Then the right, "Lightning!" When I came home, I told my mother about the fight.

14

She asked who I rooted for. I told her the white guy, as my father had instructed.

"That's wrong," she said. "You should have rooted for the American."

FISHING REPORT FOR CAPE COD BAY: Provincetown has loads of squid along with razor-teeth. If they come close, watch out for your tootsies. (Women and newbies seem to be victims of these free pedicures!) Luckily, medics abound on the beaches these days. (Thanks, Seashore EMTs!) Yellow pencil poppers were one thing mentioned. And Billingsgate—forgetaboutit. They were slamming them out here this week. Joe Stokes' waders filled up with water and we almost lost him. Always bring a buddy, remember! One crew said it was so good they didn't even have to troll; it was straight run-and-gun casting at breaking fish on both sides of the bar. Clark Railes from Sports Port took a nice 36-inch bass out of Barnstable Harbor, but lost one digit reeling in. That reel must have been hot! We always warn you guys to keep your fingers off the reel when landing! Too bad, Clark, but you'll enjoy that fish! Nine more fingers to go, but hope you learned your lesson. The end of June should be best, according to Captain Saltie, when the razor-teeth hit the Truro beaches, as always. It's fun to watch the tourists run! I shouldn't say this, but their blood attracts the best fish, free chum! Razor-teeth, as you know, are bony, like hake, but tasty. Careful unhooking, use pliers of course. Catch 'em up!

Missy Foos was a sweet cat who became crazed on the veterinarian's table. The vet hated to see him, even suggesting we put him down and get an orange cat which, he said, has an even temperament. On one visit, as Missy Foos squirmed and scratched, the vet failed to administer the vaccination. His partner, a young woman, said she would take charge. She grabbed Missy Foos, brought him to her office and left the door open. I could see her place him on the desk, where he immediately hunched up, his claws roiling paperwork. She kicked the door closed. We waited. Then we heard her scream, "He's peeing! He's peeing on my letters! My letters to Italy!"

In Chile, Missy Foos is the most common name for a cat. The most common name for a dog there is George Washington.

The bookstore owner said that the poet Edwin Seward had stopped in, browsed and on his way out, introduced himself, saying modestly that there were no books of his on the shelves. The owner said he wished he had some and Seward said he kept several boxes in the trunk of his Volvo. He laughed, saying he used them for ballast, weighing the car down on the slippery roads in Vermont where he skied. He brought in a box, signed them and the owner paid him five dollars a book. Seward then asked what they would sell for and when he was told ten dollars each, Seward handed the check back, picked up his books and said, "Are you joking? Are you kidding me? These are signed first editions."

The number one murderer of writers is self-importance.

Raymond Carver country: time-torn dreamers; the destitute, disgraced and floundering; broken-up couples and broken-down men.

16

Like many boys, I loved dirty words. When I heard "Home on the Range," with its line, "And never is heard a discouraging word," I went on a crusade to find discouraging words.

A mentally ill young man who shot himself in the head in a suicide attempt suffered a brain injury that apparently eliminated his phobia of germs and his obsession with washing his hands, doctors say. The .22 caliber slug destroyed the section of the brain responsible for his disabling obsessive-compulsive disorder without causing any other damage. The man, identified only as George, told his mother that his life was so wretched that he would rather die. She said, "Look, George, if your life is so wretched, just go and shoot yourself." So George went to the basement, stuck a .22 caliber rifle in his mouth and pulled the trigger. When he was transferred to the hospital, he hardly had any compulsions left, and is now a straight A student.

I visited the Church of Scientology in New York when I was in college. A woman, who was called a *clear*, sat across from me, as I held two cans attached by wires to a meter in front of her. She asked me to say everything I knew about a certain subject. When I finished one statement, she would say, "There's more." And I would continue, until I was *clear* on that issue. I found it hard to concentrate because she wore a very short skirt, had beautiful legs and kept pressing her knee to mine. I received letters from her for years, literally years, after this visit. Most were only one sentence, like, "How is your life?" and "Are you happy?" but what I remember best about my spiritual quest is the touch of her knee.

After seven years at the college, Thomas Hauser, Director of Buildings and Grounds, claimed he was fired via a one-sentence email. Staff had complained he repeatedly used ethnic slurs and had whispered to many female students that he'd like to get them on a slow boat to China.

In an interview with the school paper, Hauser said, "I went to the doctor this morning. I'm completely healthy. Except for the knife in my back."

The next day, in the midst of a storm, he was seen on Huntington Avenue, outside the campus center, hosting what he described as his retirement party. He said, "Yes, this is my sidewalk farewell send-off."

Hauser said the drink he was serving for the occasion would be the rain.

TEN DAY-TO-DAY GUIDELINES

Five proverbs for planning:

1. The shrike hunting the locust is unaware of the hawk hunting him.
2. The mouse with but one hole is easily taken.
3. In shallow waters, shrimps make fools of dragons.
4. Do not try to catch two frogs with one hand.
5. Give the bird room to fly.

Five proverbs for operations:

6. Do not insult the crocodile until you have crossed the river.
7. It is better to struggle with a sick jackass than carry the wood yourself.
8. Do not throw stones at a mouse and break the precious vase.

9. It is not the last blow of the ax that fells the tree.
10. The great executive not only brings home the bacon but also the applesauce.

Sherman Billingsley, owner of the Stork Club, became irritated whenever a member of the orchestra played a solo. "Why are the other guys just sitting there?" he said. "I'm paying for a whole band."

We rented the first floor of a triple-decker in a thickly settled section of Providence. It was peaceful until an elderly woman hung a set of wind chimes on her porch. The large metal tubes resounded loudly, becoming a topic of complaint among neighbors. One night several of them came to my door and asked me to speak with her, since she seemed to like me.

The next day, when she was sweeping her stoop, I mentioned that her new wind chimes had a lovely tone. Still, I said, some of us found the constant sound a bit bothersome. I asked if she might do something about them.

"Stop the wind?" she said. "Are you crazy?"

On my mother's ninetieth birthday, I take her and my father to lunch at Spanky's Fish House. She suffers from Alzheimer's and her broken foot is in a cast. He walks badly from a stroke. I apologize to diners as my parents brush and knock the closely aligned tables as we make our way to a booth. The meal ends with me guiding them one at a time through a rear door which leads to the parking lot, rather than going back through the restaurant. I escort my father to the car and settle him into the passenger seat when I panic that my mother will become disoriented in the few minutes she's alone. I run across the lot, rushing in under a big sign that says NOT AN ENTRANCE, and slam my forehead into the top plank of the door frame, falling backwards to the floor. As I hit the rug, three waitresses turn and yell at the same time, "This is not an entrance!"

On the drive home, my mother keeps asking, "Why are you holding your head?"

After so many years, after a whole life, I saw her again. "Why are you crying?" I asked. "I'm not," she answered. And indeed she was not crying, she was smiling at me, but age having distorted her features, joy no longer found access to her face, on which one might have also read, "Whoever does not die young will regret it sooner or later."

To philosophize is to learn how to die.

Gregory Corso stood at Allen Ginsberg's bedside as he lay dying, and said to Patti Smith, "Allen is teaching me how to die."

Crews stopped searching late this afternoon for a forty-one-year-old man who has been missing since he fell overboard from the *Provincetown II* ferry during a country-western music cruise in Boston Harbor Saturday night.

At approximately 10:45 P.M. Saturday, the Coast Guard Sector Boston was notified by the boat's captain that the man had fallen from the third deck into the water near Castle Island in South Boston.

The man, who was aboard the ship with his girl-friend, was apparently trying to climb the third deck railing when he fell, according to a statement from Bay State Cruise Company, which operates the *Provincetown II*.

The company said in its statement that interviews with passengers "indicate that the gentleman had been engaging in horseplay when he fell from the vessel. Two passengers reported trying to grab at the man to stop him from an athletic leap, scaling up the ship's railings."

A member of the ship's crew also tried in vain to stop the man from rambling up the railing, the company said.

The man has not been publicly identified.

The ferry was traveling at five miles per hour, when the man fell into the harbor, and was carrying 370 passengers and twenty-one crew members. The *Provincetown II* has the capacity to accommodate up to 1,100 passengers. Its weekend music cruises are marketed on the company's Facebook page as "the wildest, largest parties on the water."

Comments posted by readers of the article:

You can't cure stupid, but you can drown it.

Darwin: 1   / Drunk Country Music Fan: 0

Had this poor soul been smoking pot there would be a hue and cry to find the source of the drugs and smear the dangers of marijuana all over the front page. Alas, it was the most dangerous and destructive, albeit legal, of substances in our communities—demon alcohol.

Why would you blame alcohol rather than country music?

We shouldn't abuse God's creatures. You must reverse the haiku, not:

> A dragonfly,
> remove its wings—
> pepper tree.

but:

> A pepper tree,
> add wings to it—
> dragonfly.

An assistant professor in our department who was coming up for tenure visited my office to discuss his prospects. He had published a "found poem," which was part of a menu from Denny's, and an article on fish imagery in *Lawrence of Arabia*. I told him it didn't look good. A week later, he told me of his new plan to write a book called *The Lives of the Poets for Children*. He thought it would sell very well to parents who listen to Public Radio and want their children to be cultured. He read aloud the first sentence of two entries: Robert Frost was a grouch. Emily Dickinson hid things under her bed. He said he might not need tenure if the book made money.

A Siamese cat can be heard to say no, but never yes.

The Cape Cod hot spot, the Shipwreck Lounge, is now IN, and all kewl people know it. Come to: The Shipwreck Lounge, Hyannis, every Saturday night. You can't miss it because it's right at the end of Sea Street between the RR tracks and the harbor. Be sure to bring your sense of humor plus carry a weapon.

I asked a friend of mine, the ex-police chief of Wren-tham, if I should check it out, and this is what he said:

Definitely check out the Shippy. Instead of kara-oke, The Shipwreck has the traditional blinds hiding contest Saturdays at 11 P.M. sharp. You peek out from behind some special blinds and the patrons try to guess who you are. Right now, the town hiding champion is someone named Mr. Davis, so he is the one to beat. Besides that, The Shipwreck has a cussing, farting and nose-picking triathlon you can watch or even enter yourself. Davis, the Merv Griffin of scat, thought it up by himself, and it starts right after blinds peeking.

Sure, they thought I was a federal agent for some reason (not kidding, overheard a few people make comments) but that doesn't make it a bad place. I like to hear Bobby Darin croon "Mack the Knife" as much as the next guy (although five times in one hour may be a tad excessive). I guess I should have kept my thoughts to myself too about Patti Page. All the beer is served in plastic cups, no glasses or bottles. And just before Sunday morning arrives, they do re-enactments of the *Reservoir Dogs* "torture-me-all-you-want" scene in the basement (don't ask why I was poking around down there).

You might think you're in a home for the blind because so many creeps wear shades. Everyone in glasses not dark was called Four Eyes or Professor. When the Sox are on, and they start to lose, a habitual nitwit whistles the theme from *The Bridge on the River Kwai*. This annoyed someone who yanked the guy's Sox cap over his eyes and it stayed like that all night. He couldn't see a thing, looked weird.

The bartender sold me a cigarette lighter and I felt forced to make the buy because he said his little daughter had polio. Later, he asked me for a light and took it back and kept it. I saw him sell it to someone else, pulling the same stunt. But what could I do? I was thinking of the little girl.

Forget it, Jake. It's Chinatown.

HEADLINE: BUS-TED! COPS NAB ESCAPED KILLER ON HIGHWAY

A convicted murderer who skipped out on parole and was trying to flee the state was pulled off a crowded bus on Interstate 93 bound for South Station in a dramatic arrest "right out of a movie," the *Herald* has learned.

Joel Schmidt, 49, was arrested after state police pulled over a startled Plymouth & Brockton line bus driver nearing Exit 15 in South Boston about 1 P.M. yesterday.

Schmidt, who walked away from an East Boston halfway house Jan. 12, already had evaded police Wednesday night when they showed up at the Yarmouth home of a man he had met through a personal ad, sources said.

Yesterday, he was not as lucky.

"He gave Yarmouth police a fake ID so he was not grabbed," said one high-ranking state police source. "They went back to the house this morning, but the roommate said he jumped on a bus in Hyannis with every intention of fleeing the state from South Station."

Schmidt, convicted of second-degree murder in the 1980s and paroled in September, was removed from the bus without incident, said Sgt. Scott Range, spokesman for the Massachusetts State Police. He was booked at the South Boston barracks on charges of violating his parole.

Schmidt had served nearly 20 years in prison for repeatedly stabbing a 24-year-old Newton man in the head and heart with a kitchen knife in 1985.

He and the victim did not know each other before the killing but had ended up at a Watertown apartment with women they had met in a bar and began arguing over who would sleep where, a fight that ended in the death of Barron Giles, Middlesex County prosecutors said.

Schmidt was convicted of second-degree murder in November 1986 and sentenced to life in prison, but he became eligible for parole after 15 years.

He served nearly two decades and was released to an East Boston halfway house, a drug rehabilitation program that he fled, said Kathy Shannon, Parole Board director. An arrest warrant in his name was issued two days later, she said.

I was on that bus, a terrible bus line; the vehicles are old, cold in winter and hot in summer. Fumes often rise from the engine into the coach which holds its forty-seven passengers so tightly that the back of the seat in front of you almost rests in your lap. As we approached downtown Boston on I-93, the bus was surrounded by four state police cars, sirens on and lights swirling. Our driver pulled to the shoulder. The regular passengers, such as myself, thought the police must have spotted a flat tire or smoking engine, a common occurrence with this fleet, but why so many cars? As soon as the driver opened the door, five state troopers entered and rushed down the aisle, the lead trooper pointing to each male passenger and yelling, "ID from you! ID from you! ID from you!" and the troopers behind him inspected each one. One man stood to retrieve a briefcase from the overhead rack and the trooper slammed him into his seat. I was in the back and when the trooper reached my row, he skipped me but continued to call for the IDs of the others.

The trooper grabbed one guy and frisked him against the door to the bathroom; as he did, he nodded to two officers to seize the man in the seat behind me. The trooper told him to stand, took his ID and led him off the bus.

The trooper apologized to the man he frisked, explaining, "I needed a decoy while we got the guy we wanted."

As our bus got back on the road, the driver announced that police radioed him about a convicted murderer on the bus and told him the cops would make an arrest at the station. But they decided he was too dangerous, so they took action on the highway. The driver's voice was nervous but ecstatic, an adventure had been gained and the whole bus, usually so quiet in early morning, began to buzz.

26

I wondered: Why didn't he ask for my ID?

Later that day, in the English department hallway, I told the story to my colleagues. One guessed it was my suit and tie, but I said many others were dressed for work this way. Another asked: "Too old?" No, the escapee was my age. "What were you reading?" asked another. I pulled the textbook from the top of the shopping bag. There, on the cover, in large letters stood the title: *Poets Teaching Poets*.

My father attended a special meeting of the Knights of Columbus designed to help members convey the facts of life to their pre-adolescent sons. He returned with several typed pages which I found on my dresser the next day:

In His infinite wisdom God placed in the parents' own bodies the instruments and the materials for making an image of Himself, fashioning their bodies in such a way that in the marital embrace the husband's generative organ fits into that of his wife. And in His infinite love, God ordained that, as a climax to that loving embrace, the precious germ of life is transmitted from husband to wife united with a similar substance in her womb for the formation of a tiny human body. In the very same instant that those two elements, the father cell and the mother cell, unite in an eternal embrace to form a body, God creates in it an immortal soul, thus making a living image of Himself, an indestructible link between husband and wife, and an everlasting memorial of their mutual love.

And thus you see, my son, what a wonderful and sacred act the marital embrace is, and what an intimate union God establishes through it between Himself and human nature, between husband and wife, and between parents and their beloved child.

Renoir said, "If God had not created woman's flesh, I would never have been a painter." He ordered his wife to choose maids according to how their bodies *caught the light.*

While we live, let us live.

Charlie Frazier's father, a detective, belonged to the Whitestone Boat Club, and he took Charlie there every Saturday. One weekend, they invited me. I had heard a lot about his speedboat, the *Jo-Fran,* and was thrilled when we parked at the club, which consisted of two bathhouses, and a bar that smelled of stale beer and full ashtrays. Little pine planks on the walls had sayings like, "If You're So Schmartt, Why Ain't You Rich?" and "Kissin' Don't Last. Cookin' Do." The doors to the restrooms were marked Buoys and Gulls.

Mr. Frazier drank Rheingold with men who ridiculed the club next door, the Cresthaven Yacht Club, for putting on airs. He introduced us to a distant cousin of Chuck Connors, star of the TV show, *The Rifleman.* We were ten and impressed. Mr. Frazier gave Charlie a little tap on the rear and told us to beat it.

We wandered down the dock and along the shore which was overlooked by a large public swimming pool from which the song "Pretty Little Angel Eyes" played over and over from a juke box. I saw strange things drifting in the water and grabbed one. I was examining it at arm's length when a voice from the pool fence yelled, "Hey guys! This kid's picked up a *scumbag*!" I immediately tossed the condom into the water and stared at the teenager who wore a tight black bathing suit with a black comb stuck under it, next to his thigh.

In the clubhouse, the men had switched to whiskey and were playing tag with young women from the pool, chasing them around the bar and into the bathhouses. Mr. Frazier gave Charlie money for the hot dog vendors down the block, and then disappeared into a cabana with a girl.

When Mr. Frazier was totally drunk, he took us in the *Jo-Fran* for a midnight cruise. Under the Whitestone Bridge we dove into water among bobbing hamburger buns, cellophane wrappers and little brown spheres Charlie called *dreckies*, before heading back to the club where we got in the car.

We were stopped by the police on the way home due to Mr. Frazier's erratic driving, but his detective's ID got us off the hook. The cop said that Mr. Frazier's inspection sticker was out of date, and Mr. Frazier said he knew, and that's because he didn't have a horn, or rather, he had one, but it was in the trunk. They both laughed and the cop said good night. Mr. Frazier seemed suddenly aware that I might report the whole day to my parents and asked me to change places with Charlie and take the front seat. Charlie sat behind his father on the driver's side, and we got back on the highway. Mr. Frazier told me dirty jokes about a stripper named Lickety Split and I tried to grin. He made a deep rumbling sound in his nose and chest, gathering a huge plug of mucus which he spit out the window. It blew back into the car, hitting Charlie full in the face. Charlie began to cry and I learned another word. *Lungie.*

Mr. Frazier handed his son a napkin over the seat and we drove home in silence.

When he parked in front of my building to let me out, Mr. Frazier asked, "Do you like boating, John?"

The good sailor is known in bad weather.

When the science teacher explained that the world is round, a student asked, "Then why aren't people falling off?"

The teacher answered, "They are. They're falling off all the time."

Pluck your magic twanger, Froggie.

Littlewood's Law of Miracles states that in the course of any normal person's life, miracles happen at a rate of roughly one per month. The proof of the law is simple. During the time that we are awake and actively engaged in living our lives, roughly for eight hours each day, we see and hear things happening at a rate of about one per second. So the total number of events that happen to us is about thirty thousand per day, or about a million per month. With few exceptions, these events are not miracles because they are insignificant. The chance of a miracle is about one per million events. Therefore we should expect about one miracle to happen, on the average, every month.

Over Carl Jung's door: *VOCATUS ADQUE NON VOCATUS, DEUS ADERIT.* CALLED OR NOT CALLED, GOD IS PRESENT.

I'm not sure I learned a thing that whole year under Sister Sheila Gay. Didn't we spend eighth grade writing "I will not talk" five hundred times? Patty Picozzi was feeling the Christmas spirit and wrote her punishment in the shape of a Christmas tree. Sister Sheila nearly had a coronary and pulled her up out of her seat by her long red braid and sent her to Sister Renee. I remember thinking how lucky she was to get out of the classroom.

I was talking when I shouldn't have been and Sister Gay led me to the front of the classroom and dumped me into the trash can. I had to sit there until lunch time. The worst thing about it was that she had thrown out roses with thorns in them and they scratched the back of my legs. It was the only time my mom went to school to complain.

We decided to play an April Fool's joke and instead of singing the national anthem, we sang "I Think I Love You" by Bobby Sherman. We also wore two different shoes on our feet. We all agreed to do this but when the time came I was the only one out of uniform and singing with all my heart. Of course I got the ruler across my rear.

When the woodmen entered the forest, the trees said, "The ax is one of us."

Dear Faculty,

If you have not yet completed your midterm grade submissions, please note that you must do so by October 26th at 12:00 noon ET. There are no extensions. If you have any questions, please email the Registrar.

Sincerely,
The Registrar

P.S. If you are finished submitting midterm grades/reporting classes for which you have no midterm grades to submit, please disregard this message.

Monica sat at the ocean's edge reading *Lolita*. She didn't notice the rising tide until it almost crashed over her.

Judith sat in a lawn chair in her front yard reading Frank Harris's *My Life and Loves*. She didn't notice that her baby boy had crawled over the grass, across the sidewalk and was on all fours in the middle of the road.

Everything must be learned, from reading to dying.

The painter and printmaker Judy Shahn, whose precisely drafted works were known for their craftsmanship, received a phone call one day at home.

"I'm calling to say I really love your paintings," the voice said. "Don't hang up."

"I won't," she said.

"I'm crazy about them," he said. "I just can't explain it."

"Thank you very much," she said.

"Don't hang up," he said.

"I won't," she said.

"They're really beautiful," he said.

"Tell me," she said, "where have you seen my paintings?"

"*Paintings*?" he said. "I said *panties*!"

Spray-painted on the trestle of the Long Island Railroad in bright red lettering was: *Delaney and Kerrie L.A.M.F.* It was a sign of deep commitment. No one dared flirt with Kerrie, since she and Delaney were together *Like A Mother Fucker.*

You're asking to be my friend—or whatever this is? Friend you? This after you completely ignored my contribution to the department over all those years—not even a peep about me, but meanwhile praising Marty Rife and a number of morons who contributed one tenth of what I did to the curriculum? Not to mention inspiring you to take up rock climbing, which probably added years to your life? Are you kidding?

I'll be dead, you'll be dead, we'll all be dead.

The boy, taken by his parents across South America, stood at the top of a mountain and screamed, "Oh no! Not another vista!"

Life is, after all, just one person after another.

May I bone your kipper, *mademoiselle*?

Customer reviews and a police report about the International Inn's Cuddle & Bubble in Hyannis:

> We turned on our Jacuzzi—within three minutes the water was BROWN. It took an hour for someone to come up to our room, and he told us that it was our own dead skin that was the culprit. I had a rash that persisted for two days.

> The inn keeper on duty said he heard screaming from the room and when he entered, he saw a guest smoking, which is prohibited in the inn. The guest assaulted him with the ironing board by charging into him, pushing him into the hallway and pinning him to the wall.

> First of all, I'm a flexible lady. I enjoy fine dining and expensive travel as much as the next girl, but I'm a camper at heart. I am no snoot about accommodations and I knew this was going to be a dive motel and I was excited. I didn't even consider going to CVS for some bleach like my friends had done in the past. So let's get into it. The couple who got there right before us walked into their room and walked right back out for a refund (which the manager refused to give them). They said the handles on the hot tub were brown and the room was nasty. They had driven three hours to stay there and REFUSED to stay the night.
>
> Obviously, this had us SUPER excited to see our room. Which took us two more tries because they first gave us keys that didn't work and then they forgot to give us bubbles.

Two long walks in the freezing cold was super annoying, especially when you just wanna pop some champagne and get naked.

Luckily for us (and for the fact we were only going to be there for three hours) the hot tubs worked. The room was absolutely TINY though and turned into a sauna within ten minutes of using the hot tub (and required A/C and an open window to breathe).

The rest of the place was pretty much a disaster. We were brave enough to get full use out of the jacuzzi but refused to put our bare feet in their shower.

THE GOOD NEWS: You couldn't actually hear anyone having sex. Considering it was Valentine's Day, I was impressed (and comforted) by the fact that they've got some good soundproofing going on.

Police arrested Joseph Gilberti for assault with a dangerous weapon, using a plastic champagne glass to cut his girlfriend during an argument in the jacuzzi.

Dear Professor:

Hello, would you be willing to write a letter of recommendation? I took the course Advanced Creative Writing: Poetry. This letter is for my application to Jeju Graduate School located in an island south of mainland Korea. I will be applying to the school of Philosophy.

In your class I remained fairly quiet but hopefully produced poems you'll remember:

"Come as Your Favorite Dead Relative Costume
    Party"
"O Mr. Yogi Bear"
"The Priest and The Paperboy"
"Lord Forgive Me"
"The Egg and Uncle"

Your former student,
Bertrand

I thanked the electrician as he left our house. He asked, "Are you John Skoyles, the writer?" Shocked to be recognized, I said I was.

"So those are all your books stacked next to the fuse box?"

Answer that and stay fashionable!

Doctor, my eyes
Tell me what is wrong
Was I unwise to leave them open for so long

The Yorktown area of New York City was once crowded with German restaurants. My aunt took me to the Jaeger House, where the waiter proudly described the menu in a thick accent. After a long list, he pronounced, in a deep, stentorian voice that was unforgettable: "These are the schnitzels."

Never eat more in a single day than your head weighs.

Letter to the Faculty:

Welcome to Fall! Why is it that summer passes so quickly? Before we get into the fast pace of the new semester, I want to take a few minutes of your time.

1.) Dean's List: Too many of our students place on the Dean's List, so Faculty Assembly endorsed increasing the grade point average needed to 3.70 or higher.

2.) Assessing Assessment: ever wonder what keeps a chief academic officer awake at night? The answer for this one is: Are we really making a difference in the lives of our students? Are we putting together the right classes to help them become better critical thinkers? How do we know? There are many ways of looking at assessment, but how do we assess assessment? This past year, our Associate VP has devoted time and thought to this area. He attended three conferences on the subject and so I have appointed him Chair of the Assessing Assessment Committee and he will be asking for volunteers shortly.

3.) Promoting Civility: strange that this topic would appear in a letter like this, but many times this past year, I have heard of student behaviors that, to put it mildly, are simply rude and uncivil. The challenges of teaching are sufficient to occupy us. It is truly disturbing to learn that students take the joy out of teaching by displaying unacceptable behaviors ranging from text messaging to playing Internet games in class to sending faculty members letters with language un-publishable in any daily newspaper. The library staff just completed the College Library Code of Conduct for distribution to all students who come into that area. This is an important first step.

4.) The name Continuing Education (CE) has been changed to Professional Studies and Special Programs (PSSP).

I look forward to working with you as we explore shared governance and learn from one another of the various ways we can support each other's efforts.

The Dean

These are the schnitzels.

Derek, the poet, closed his eyes and said, "Poetry gives us ourselves."

Picasso and Braque were rivals. Both had followings of young artists, each devoted to their masters. The two often discussed trading paintings and one day it was done. Braque visited Picasso's studio, chose the most exquisite painting he could find, and placed it over his fireplace, telling his students it was a gift from Picasso. Picasso went to Braque's studio and left with the ugliest, most wretched painting of Braque's, and displayed it similarly for his students.

Judy Shahn reported the phone call about her panties to the police. A cop visited her house, took a look around and told her not to hang her laundry on the line for a few weeks.

I gave a reading in New York City with a poet who introduced his poem about baseball as being for men only. He said, "I think you have to have genitalia to understand this poem."

A friend of James Merrill complained that his opium habit had made him impotent. Merrill replied, "Poppycock!"

It was the week after Easter as I walked under the Roosevelt Avenue elevated train and saw on the top of a full litter basket, a rabbit cowering from trains overhead and the noise of passing cars. An Easter gift, a reminder of spring and that Christ has risen.

Mr. Lobelli, our fifth grade teacher, weighed nearly 400 pounds and threw erasers at the head of any student talking when he wanted quiet. Once in a while he slammed the wrong kid in the face. A cloud of chalk dust and a bloody nose was cause for a weak apology. He used to exit and enter the classroom door sideways, he was so large. I checked out his belt at a rehearsal for *The Sound of Music*—a 62-inch waist.

He placed his desk near the window he kept open because he smoked: one menthol, followed by one regular.

He had a long-standing feud with Miss Prentiss. One day she stomped into our classroom and began an argument, saying he knew none of our names. She challenged him to name just one boy out of the forty of us, but he couldn't—he called each of us "Sonny." They yelled at each other, louder and fiercer while the class watched. Finally, she left, but turned at the door and called him a faggot. Mr. Lobelli said, "Why don't you plaster up your vagina, you'll never use it again."

Many people won't kill themselves for fear of what their neighbors will say.

The gardening expert, Felice Quinto, addressed the women's flower club during a winter so mild that buds opened in late February. A club member wondered if a spring snow would damage this new growth. Mr. Quinto explained that it would not, that the snow would provide insulation to the young and tender shoots. He said it was similar to the way that, during sex, pubic hair acts as a dry lubricant.

The local newspaper calls me annually to ask for a comment on the winner of the Nobel Prize in literature. Most of the time, I haven't heard of the writer. After getting tired of confessing my ignorance, I say, year after year, to their perfect satisfaction, and which they repeatedly quote, "Long overdue."

English playwright Joe Orton and his partner stole and doctored library books as a prank, then re-shelved them in the stacks. They replaced Poet Laureate John Betjeman's body on the dust jacket with a tattooed man in bikini briefs, and added new titles to the table of contents of *The Collected Plays of Emlyn Williams,* including "Knickers Must Fall" and "Fucked by Monty." A portrait of Hedda Hopper covered an English professor's author photo. They were sentenced to six months in prison.

I guarded the King of Sweden at a Christmas pancake breakfast for the Boy Scouts, and one of the king's retinue asked me to feed the reindeer. A clumsy waitress spilled a tray of Swedish meatballs on the king's lap. Then a reindeer got loose and knocked over the smorgasbord table, but that wasn't my fault. My task was to feed the reindeer not to hold them. But I got in trouble because they eat cherry soup and I forgot to wipe their chins and so they scared some Cub Scouts who thought it was blood. But tomorrow's another day!

I had been a guest at many dinner parties given by my colleagues at the college. As I lived alone, I was invited often, but had not reciprocated. So I invited three couples to my apartment for beef stew which I made from an online recipe. I found preparing the dish enjoyable. I chopped carrots, diced potatoes, browned the beef. A can of Campbell's onion soup was called for, and I had it open and ready for the pot, but after everyone had left, congratulating me on a fine dinner—one guest said it was the best beef stew she ever had—I found the full can on the counter. I was certain I had put it in. I consoled myself, reassured that the stew was a success without it, but when I was cleaning up, I found an empty Campbell's can in the trash, the one I had kept on the stove for months, filling it with grease.

To save money, the Dean hired Zinvoy Rostov, a stout Russian immigrant and former professional wrestler, to teach mathematics. He was wealthy and refused a salary. His office was on my hall, and often, when I looked up from my desk, I caught him peeking in and darting off. One day he entered, sat across from me and asked if I would critique his verse play. The play, written in couplets, concerned two men stranded on an island. When we met a week later, it was clear he wanted only praise. He asked if I had admired his command of rhyme, the exact rhymes he used in every couplet. I had to say that many of the rhymes were not exact. I guessed his accent had distorted them. He grew very resentful and puffed up his shoulders as if for a take-down. He refuted every poor rhyme I showed him, saying, "Find another example!" This went on for five minutes, and when I pointed out the lines—

> *How sad to be trapped on this island with my pal,*
> *without a woman, or even a brothel—*

he stood up, indignant and said, "Couldn't it be *broth-al*?"

I said a more exact rhyme would be "gal," but I tried to buck him up, saying he was onto something with his rhyme for orange even though inexact. He had used "foreign," which I complimented.

"That's nothing," he said. "I can give you a million rhymes for orange!" And then he listed them, counting his rhyming words on each of his fingers, "Torrange! Forrange! Morrange! Porrange!"

Buy the best and cry once.

When James Merrill sent a rhyming dictionary to Agha Shahid Ali, he enclosed a note that said, "Let this be our little secret."

Squid stew is a dish loved by poets and artists. I first had squid stew at the Portuguese restaurant, Cookie's Tap. Cookie's in Provincetown was the hangout of numerous local characters like Howard Mitcham, a chef whose seafood cookbooks have been praised by Anthony Bourdain. Howard had a special booth at Cookie's for himself and Herman, his pet quahog. Deaf, he often communicated by writing on the disposable towels from the men's room. I have his poem, "Song of the Humpback Whale," inscribed on that rough brown paper. Another regular was artist Jackson Lambert, who was at work on his autobiography, *Squid Row*.

Tomas Tranströmer visited Provincetown, and loved Cookie's. There we discussed Montale's first book, *Ossi di seppia (Cuttlefish Bones)*, the cuttlefish being a close relative of the squid. One day he happily announced he had found the perfect dinner: "Squid stew and an order of fava beans!"

Many artists used squid ink, a beautiful sepia color. And one, Paul Bowen, made the best stew around, with fresh squid he caught at the end of MacMillan Wharf in the middle of the night. I have tried numerous recipes over the years, and the one I offer here is the result of a combination of many of them.

Recipe

3 pounds squid
3 onions, chopped

4 cloves of garlic, minced
1 can of tomatoes (28 ounce), crushed
2 carrots, diced
1 cup mushrooms, chopped
2/3 cup olive oil
1 tsp crushed red pepper
1 cup red wine
2 tbsp vinegar
1 tsp salt

You might be able to buy squid already cleaned. If not, a 3 pound box is available in the frozen fish section of the supermarket. Thaw, then cut in front of the eye—be aware that the ink can squirt out forcefully—I have splattered many shirts and walls this way. This cut separates the tentacles from the body. Remove the beak, which is at the center of the tentacles, and discard. Take a small piece of paper towel and grab the "pen" – a long clear piece of cartilage—from the body, and discard. Do not try to write with it.

Run water over the squid until they are thoroughly clean. Wash tentacles as well. Next, slice the squid. I like to cut the squid into both rings and into two inch lengths; this gives a variation to the meat. If the tentacles are large, cut them in half. Throw away the two longest tentacles.

In a large sauce pot, sauté the onion and garlic, then add everything else, bring to boil, lower heat and simmer for 3 hours. Add water if you like a thinner mix. The stew is even better the next day.

Wallace Stevens was a formal man with a vaudevillian sense of humor. Each time he travelled from Connecticut, where he was Vice President of the Hartford Insurance Company, to Philadelphia, to review that branch, the employees there dreaded his arrival. He loved hot cross buns, buying them by the dozen at the train station and bringing them to the meeting. Sitting at the head of the table, he passed the bags around, insisting everyone take one. He never brought napkins and the employees sat through the afternoon, each with a handful of goo.

Stevens laughed only to himself over this prank— no confederate, no friend or sidekick to share the joke.

When his chauffeur, Naaman Corn, took him to Hartt College of Music for an honorary Doctor of Humanities degree, the driver said, "I figured a humanitarian award should be given to somebody that had done something for humanity. Goodness alive, looks like they could have picked on somebody else."

We adopted a kitten from the pound for our six-year-old daughter, and it turned out to be a mean one. It scratched and bit us without cause. When our daughter lifted her kitten to show her friend, it held up a threatening claw and hissed. The friend asked, "Why no meow?"

A poem has a beginning, a middle and an end, but not necessarily in that order.

We lived in a suburban town where the neighbors regularly attended church. The couple across the street noticed our cars in the driveway on Sunday, and the wife once asked us in an accusatory tone, "What are you, Jewish?"

When I had brain surgery for an acoustic neuroma, I returned from the hospital with large staples running up the side of my shaved head. At the same time, my wife's father was dying and she left to be with him. I needed to refill the prescription to alleviate my headaches, but I couldn't drive as my balance nerve had been removed and I couldn't even walk with any stability. I called the religious woman across the street to ask her to take me to the drug store, which she generously did. And generous, too, were the other customers who moved aside on seeing the ghastly scar, allowing me the front of the line. When my neighbor dropped me off at home, I thanked her and she said, "That pain almost makes you want to believe in God, doesn't it?"

"Almost," I said.

Forrest Mars, who invented M & Ms, Milky Way, Three Musketeers and Snickers, had an obsession with perfection, a zealot's fervor and a terrible temper. Rising in the middle of the night to open a packet of M & Ms, he inspected the candy discs and, if he found the initials printed even slightly off center, he'd call the factory manager and demand the candy be recalled. At meetings, he would fall to his knees, clasping his hands, and say to the sky, "I pray for Snickers! I pray for Milky Way!"

Love is born of admiration and not of pity.

I bought my first house, in Asheville, North Carolina, the oldest and cheapest house in a good neighborhood. It was on a full acre and, a few days after we moved in,

I walked the property, discovering the sound of a trickling stream at the foot of the hill in the back. I couldn't believe I owned land with such a marvel. I followed the sound to its source, water running down the side of the embankment. Then I noticed something in the water—long yellow strands, linguini, the remnants of last night's dinner down the garbage disposal, cascading from a broken sewer pipe.

On Bring Your Pet to Work Day, the dean's assistant brought her kitten, Shalom, to the office. It immediately danced away sideways and hid. The secretaries, the associate dean, and the student workers walked the halls and looked under desks, calling, "Shalom! Shalom!" The dean came out of her office, obligated to pitch in, but instead of calling the cat's name, she cupped her hand to her mouth and called, "Shoah! Shoah!" The word, not for peace, but for the holocaust.

Allen Grossman gave a series of lectures entitled, "Poetry: A Basic Practice," to a general audience at the Smithsonian. The first lecture defined poetry as "the art that allows a success for everyone at the limits of the autonomy of the will to effect its purposes by other means."

It was snowing, and it was going to snow.

When you buy a book on Amazon, you receive suggestions for similar reading under the heading: *Customers who bought this item also bought...* A volume by a heady author might result in a list of books by Hannah Arendt, James Baldwin or Octavio Paz.

I ordered some copies of my own books for an event, along with a few items for my daughter. A week later, I needed more copies and, when I went to the site, I found this heading next to my book: *Customers who made this purchase also bought The Stir Crazy Popcorn Popper.*

Robert T. Nelson sold a brass cylinder containing virilium to be hung around the neck or placed in the buttonhole. He claimed it would kill bacteria twenty feet from the wearer through its radioactive properties. These "magic spikes" sold for hundreds of dollars, and were worn by politicians and celebrities. The government took him to court, proving that virilium was actually rat poison and not radioactive in any way. Nelson said his product was an "unrecognized form of radioactivity."

Dumplings in a dream are not dumplings, but a dream.

Higgins head-butted a tournament director, threatened to shoot a fellow snooker player even though they were on the same team, and punched a referee during a charity match.

> White shoes
> White hat
> Black shirt
> Cadillac
> The boy's a time bomb.

Don't lead with your chin.

Miles Davis gave a concert at Fairfield University in the late sixties when I was a student. His band played for an hour without him and the crowd booed and jeered until someone pushed Miles on stage from a side curtain. He aimed his trumpet toward the roof of the field house, blew one long note and fell face first to the floor. A few weeks later, Segovia played and was interrupted by someone coughing uncontrollably. Segovia removed his handkerchief and patted his lips, silently instructing the cougher to cover his mouth. Soon after, Buffalo Springfield performed with the Beach Boys, the Soul Survivors and Strawberry Alarm Clock. My roommate worked for WVOF, the Voice of Fairfield, and was recruited to perform a sound check. He said all of the groups were happy with the run-throughs, but the Strawberry Alarm Clock complained and complained and had the sound crew adjust things over and over until finally my roommate said, "Segovia was here last week, and it was fine with him."

The Alarm Clock drummer said, "Maybe Segovia doesn't give a fuck!"

You could throw a guitar off a tall, rock-strewn cliff and it would play "Gloria" all the way down.

Our retired Victorian Literature Professor was listening to a CD of Louis Armstrong teaching Lotte Lenya how to sing "Mack the Knife," and was going to give a talk on the subject to the local chorale society headed by Lotte Lenya's niece, to be held in his new auditorium.

Jack Paar interviewed Oscar Levant, the pianist, author and actor renowned for his pill-popping and neurotic behavior, and Paar asked, "Did it ever occur to you, dear old friend, that a lot of your trouble or illness may just be in your mind?"

Levant said, "What a place for it to be!"

> I don't need no doctor
> for my prescription to be filled
> (I don't need no doctor)
> (I don't need no doctor)

Professor Sadler referred to his seminar of beautiful girls as "twenty thousand volts of jailbait."

He was crying, and he was going to cry.

We were met at the door by our host's wife, Maggie, who held two silver pitchers, one with a piece of masking tape marked GIN, the other VODKA.

"Martini?" she asked.

I chose gin but my friend declined. The hostess asked again and my friend replied that he was sober. Maggie insisted until my friend finally said, "Maggie, you don't understand. I'm an alcoholic."

Maggie replied, "Oh, so am I!"

John Cheever gave the same blurb to several books: A terribly funny novel.

Pulitzer Prize winning poet Alan Dugan on teaching at Sarah Lawrence:

> A student tried to pull me on top of her
> with the door to my office closed.
> I put my hands on her buttocks,
> she put her hands on my buttocks
> and said, "Fuck off, old man."
> That memory has become a permanent part
>   of my soul.

Survived by his wife.

I had dinner with Allen Grossman and his wife Judith at Henrietta's Table. Judith ordered tuna, rare, but when it arrived, it was overdone. She mentioned this to the waiter, who brought the manager to our table. He apologized profusely, saying, "There is nothing worse in the world than overdone tuna!"

Allen said, "It must be a very happy world then."

My doctor ordered an MRI of my brain to see if a tumor was responsible for the ringing in my ear. At the end of the first round of images, the technician who administered the procedure said there was nothing there, and I rejoiced as he injected dye to get a clearer picture. When that was over he said, "Oh, there *is* a tumor."

I drove home, stopping for a drink at a place called Louie's Beer Stadium. The bartender told me the stadium was a private club and I had to be a member in order to be served. He apologized, saying the county was dry, and the club was a way around the law.

"Although you could be a guest…" he said, nodding to a member leaning over a gin and tonic.

The patron did not look up, but simply said, "He's my guest."

I had to sign a register, and then I bought a drink for myself and for my host before going off to a table to contemplate the tumor in a world where everything seemed either host or guest.

C - that's the way to begin
H - that's the next letter in
I - that is the third
C - time to season up the bird
K - I'm fitting in
E - getting near the
N
C-H-I-C-K-E-N
That's the way to spell chicken.

To the Editor:

What a shame! That an obituary begins by referring to a man as the Town Drunk!

I knew "Iron Man" since we were kids and the anecdotes are probably true, but he quit like he started, on his own because he wanted to.

Editor replies: Mr. Joseph was indeed the town drunk, far worse than any on our streets today.

To the Editor:

Starting out the article by calling Francis the town drunk was very upsetting to his family. Also, by saying he did not know how to read or write was absolutely incorrect.

Editor replies: A long-time close friend of Francis told us that Francis could not read, providing many details to support that claim. Please notice that we were told he was very proud of having sobered up. Everyone was proud of him for that, including us. That's why his obit was so good.

He died beyond his means.

In high school, I used to lie in bed with a transistor radio under my pillow, listening to the talk show host, Long John Nebel, at midnight. Most of his guests were members of the occult: one believed that the Deros, short for Detrimental Robots, lived far under the earth, accessible through a special elevator in New York, which would plunge down three miles to their world if you pressed the basement button twice. Others had been abducted by aliens, travelled in flying saucers, or owned four-hundred-pound dogs from Pluto. One had made love to a six-inch blonde. Long John answered the phones until dawn, and some nights caller after caller would blast him as a dumb and stupid phony. These sometimes went on for a half hour, and I wondered how so many people could hate him so much, although he did try my patience too, like the time he took twenty minutes to tell the story of returning an electric blanket to Macy's. Nebel, in turn, would insist his tormentors did not bother him, even as he called them yellow bastards, cowards and ordered them back into their "jars of formaldehyde."

Years later, I found that all of these harassing calls were from the same two pranksters, who simply hung up and dialed continuously in different voices. Jim Nazium and Hank Hayes produced a CD called "Hello, John?"

When Prohibition ended, Ernest Gallo and his brothers, Julio and Joe, planned to corner the young wine market. Ernest wanted the company to become "the Campbell Soup company of the wine industry" so he produced a cheap wine called Thunderbird. Their radio ads played a jingle that went:

> What's the word?
> Thunderbird.
> How's it sold?
> Good and cold.
> What's the jive?
> Bird's alive.
> What's the price?
> Thirty twice.

Ernest once drove through a tough, inner city neighborhood and stopped when he saw a man standing over a burning trash can. He rolled down his window and called out, "What's the word?" The immediate answer was, "Thunderbird."

Paul Winchell, the ventriloquist who created Jerry Mahoney and Knucklehead Smiff, also invented a flameless cigarette lighter, battery-heated gloves and the invisible garter belt. The film voice of Pooh's Tigger, Winchell died within hours of John Fiedler, the voice of Pooh's Piglet.

John Skoyles Grade 2A St. Bartholomew October 9, 1956 Religion Test Grade 100%:

1. Blessed Mother
2. Dec. 8
3. Honesty
4. 10
5. Baptism

To Whom It May Concern:

I am pleased to serve as a reference for Bertrand La Ponce's application to the Masters program in philosophy at the Graduate School of Jeju National University.

He was a student of mine in Advanced Creative Writing: Poetry. His original and inventive poems, "Lord Forgive Me," "The Egg and Uncle," "The Priest and the Paperboy," "Come as Your Favorite Dead Relative Costume Party" and "O Mr. Yogi Bear" surprised me and the class. He invented something he called "the sneak-thief stanza," which was a quatrain that had almost nothing to do with the subject of the poem, but was related in an interesting way. These pieces were humorous as well as contemplative. This latter quality is what makes me feel that he would be an excellent candidate for an advanced degree in philosophy at Jeju National University.

I met Richard Sewall, the famed biographer of Emily Dickinson. He had taught at Yale for more than forty years and told me about his course called, Daily Themes. I asked which themes were most memorable and he answered without hesitation those written by soldiers returning to school after WWII. One soldier wrote that he was in charge of a barge filled with Japanese prisoners of war. They were out at sea when he received an order to dump them. And he wrote that he did what he was told, he dumped them.

In 1947, the Squirrel Gulch district of Idaho Springs, in a fit of post-WWII patriotism, renamed itself, "Steve Canyon," as a tribute to the comic strip fighter pilot.

Two years later, they convinced the federal government to pay the Indiana Limestone Company $12,000 to carve a larger-than-life statue of their new namesake. It was shipped to Colorado and formally dedicated on July 8, 1950. Its plaque reads, in part, "The United States Treasury salutes Steve Canyon and, through him, all American cartoon characters who serve our Nation."

Cartoonist Milton Caniff, who created Steve Canyon, played no part in the tribute, but "in appreciation for his enthusiasm," Idaho Springs gave him a gold mine.

In 1965, when I was sixteen, I bought a paperback of Sappho's lyrics, translated by Willis Barnstone. The introduction said, "It is no longer news to say that human beings are *normally* more or less bisexual…" I showed the book to my father. A man who never finished fifth grade, and who had been an airplane mechanic, a first class petty officer in WWII and, finally, an envelope salesman, he replied that he thought it was true but that I should never mention it to anyone.

> Let there be light
> Let the games begin

Let me take a look
Let the sun shine in
Let the little girl dance
Let him alone
Let sleeping dogs lie
Let him have it
Let's get out of here
Let me go
Let the bells of freedom ring
Let me be
Let us pray
Let him go free
Let's get together
Let's spend the night together
Let's dance
Let me kick out the jams
Let bygones be bygones
Let it be
Let it bleed

I'd been thinking about something that I found in your work and Guston's. It struck me that so much good and meaningful work, literary and visual, shares a particular characteristic. In yours and in Guston there is a meeting of the comic and the painful or, in his case, the comical and the dangerous or the simply comical and sad when it comes to his images of himself. I suppose a quick way of saying it would be to use the word *poignancy*, which can mean that, but sometimes is diminished by a certain sentimentality. So much of your language seems to me to be born out of these seemingly conflicting emotions. They speak the truth of the world's complexity, heightened. In the Guston it is true as well. He later developed images of the Klan figures into buffoons, yet always dangerous buffoons.

Q. Where is child prodigy writer Barbara Newhall Follett? She wrote *The House without Windows* when she was eleven years old. I understand that she grew up in Brookline and disappeared one day. Did she ever return?

A. Apparently not. Barbara was deeply unhappy. At the age of fifteen, she ran away from her parents' home in Pasadena, and when tracked by detectives to a San Francisco hotel, she tried to kill herself by jumping out a window. Her parents later separated and Barbara's own early marriage foundered. Living in Brookline, she worked as a secretary and hated it. She was last seen on December 7, 1939, leaving her Brookline apartment with $30 and a shorthand pad.

Our paychecks bore the statement: *There are no unimportant people on jobs at Warren Wilson College.*

What we propose is an anthology of poems that imagine the later experiences—the afterlife, as it were—of famous characters from literature—what happened to Prufrock after the tea party? To Ishmael when he finally made it back to terra firma? To the speaker and neighbor in Frost's "Mending Wall" after they finish the job? You get the idea...

All the guests were directed to the stretch of beach outside Norman Mailer's house on the bay, so that his widow, Norris, could address us from the deck about plans for the foundation in Norman's name. The organizers forgot to consult the tides, and the tide was rising, so what we heard of Norris's speech went like this—"I'm so happy that you all could... WHOOSH, WHOOSH..." and "Norman would be so pleased that we want to preserve the WHOOSH..."

No one will read it unless you put zombies in it.

The Zombies Ron Argent went on to found Argent.

Dear John,

    I understand you have published a book of personal essays. I would like to publicize this accomplishment in the next issue of Alumni News. Please call me to acknowledge you received this. I called your home twice and the woman on the other end hung up on me both times.

Shelley Matthew
Editor, Alumni News

On the grave of a local artist: NOT FORGOTTEN BECAUSE NEVER KNOWN.

From *The Provincetown Banner*: "Mark Doty, a Provincetown poet, won the National Book Critics Circle Award for *My Alexandria*. Doty moved to Provincetown in 1990 from Vermont, with his partner Wallace Stevens, who died of AIDS three weeks ago. *My Alexandria* is dedicated to Stevens. Doty wrote the poems in that book during the time when he first learned that Stevens had AIDS and until their first move to Provincetown."

The rest of the article continues to refer to "Wally," mistakenly, as Wallace Stevens.

When I saw Mark after the article was published, I mentioned not knowing that he lived with Wallace Stevens.

"I outed him," Mark said.

Zen master Gutei Oshō held up one finger when asked the meaning of Zen. It became known as One Finger Zen. When Oshō was away, a visitor asked his disciple "What is Buddhism?" The boy mimicked his master. Oshō heard about it and asked his disciple the same question. When the boy held up his finger, Oshō grabbed a cleaver and cut it off. The stunned student screamed and was running from the zendo when Oshō called his name. The boy turned, Oshō held up one finger and the disciple was immediately enlightened.

Editor's Note, *The New York Times:* An article in the Arts pages on December 26 described a reporter's efforts to find out how the magician David Copperfield performed his tricks in *Dreams and Nightmares*, the Broadway show that closed its run on December 29. The article included an interview with a man identifying himself as an audience plant who explained how the magician could make him appear to levitate on a couch twenty feet above the stage. The man, who produced ticket stubs indicating that he had been at many performances, said he was disgruntled about being paid late for his work. He identified himself as Seth Greenspan, an employee of the show, but that identification was false. After the article was published, the producer of *Dreams and Nightmares* visited the *Times* with the real Mr. Greenspan, who produced full identification. A telephone number at which the imposter was reached, after the original interview, has since been disconnected. The producer, Jonathan Hochwald, declines to discuss the accuracy of the imposter's comments about how the tricks were performed.

At a writer's conference, Francine du Plessix Gray mistook George Garrett for a bell hop, and offered him a fifty-cent tip after he brought luggage to her room. He tried to decline, but she said, "Let it be our little secret."

FROM A RESUME: Co-director, Cake Committee, 1987 Very Special Arts Festival: planned and constructed a thirty-foot large birthday cake for New Hampshire, through which a marching band and 350 candles (special needs people) stomped to meet New Hampshire's governor.

Edith Piaff, between 1951 and 1963: four car accidents, one suicide attempt, four morphine cures, one drug-induced sleeping cure, three comas from liver disease, one attack of raving madness, two of delirium tremens, seven operations, two bronchial pneumonias and a pulmonary oedema.

The least used library in the U.S. — Las Vegas.

The most attractive library staff in the U.S. — Las Vegas. Showgirls and call girls who are arrested and sent to the library to perform community service.

THE ASSOCIATED PRESS
MEMORANDUM

To: Mr. Freddie Miller

From: Mr. James Houlihan, Head of Mailroom, Associated Press

Subject: Lateness

Dear Freddie:

Your chronic lateness has not stopped. I have spoken to you about this many times. Obviously you have no intentions to stop.

Your hours are from 9:30 A.M. to 6:00 P.M., with 10 mis. coffee break twice a day, lunch has always been one (1) hour. You lateness has been in these areas mentioned in this letter.

The Assoicated Press and I will not tolerate this no longer.

JH

The Order of the Occult Hand is a whimsical secret society of American journalists who have been able to slip the meaningless and telltale phrase, "It was as if an occult hand had..." past editors and into print as a game and inside joke.

My neighbor was upset because my new driveway was parallel to his. He said that when I pulled in, he couldn't tell if someone was coming to his house or to mine. I told him that when I came home, I would honk twice so he would know it was me.

The samurai looks insignificant next to his armor of black dragon scales.

The dean asked the chair of the English Department if he would be interested in annexing the Journalism Department. The chair replied, "Journalism is what you wrap fish in the next day."

The college awarded an honorary doctor of letters degree to a renowned surgeon. At the rehearsal, the person in charge told him that when he was introduced, he should leave his seat, approach the microphone, bend slightly to receive the hood, say a few words, and then return to his seat. The sequence was then practiced, in which he received praise in the traditional second person, "You have done this and you have done that..." He spoke into the microphone, "Thank you. Thank you for the platitudes." I was impressed with his sense of humor at the run through, but when the ceremony took place a few hours later, he said the same thing.

My Aunt Mae invited me to her apartment for dinner. I had just graduated from high school and FM radio was starting to play rock music. Mae had a Silvertone in her living room on which I found the Beatles' "A Day in the Life." She served Harvey's Bristol Cream and asked me to change the station to easy listening music. I loved the song and was hesitant to do so. I had my hand on the turning knob, but the song itself includes a rising crescendo which mimics the sound of a radio dial swirled across stations, transitioning to a peppy Paul McCartney lilt which my aunt enjoyed, saying, "Oh that's so much better," although I had done nothing.

Fiction writer Walter Johnson lived with his family in Cambridge, and he often left for months at a stretch for teaching posts around the country. Each time he returned, he gave a reading from his new stories which often involved his affairs. His wife always sat front and center, surrounded by women friends, as if to buffer her from the words they were about to hear. She and her entourage entered and exited funereally, a group of mourners. They were in particular despair the night Walter read about his going to a roadhouse in San Antonio, and leaving at closing time with an overweight, toothless lady of the night. The story ended with the sentence, "I clung to her the way a man clings to a rock before he falls off a cliff."

My mother's diary:

> April 26, 1971. We replaced tube (5v46B) on the TV Ethel gave us. TV man next door said it should be replaced every year or two. $2.20. The set (picture and sound) would go off entirely—if we pressed the tube back down it would come in clear. Then it would go off again later. New tube fixed it.

> April 27, 1973. Same trouble as above. Picture came in small. Then when we turned set

on there was no picture and no sound. Tube (5v46B) did not go on. TV man (new one) next door said tube was good, must be the socket. When we jiggled it around the set went on, but after it was turned off did not come on again. Finally I lifted the tube part way up from the socket and set stayed on. Extra tube in drawer (old one). Two days later set went off again. TV man next to King Kullen said must be the socket. It spoils one prong on tube. Set would have to be taken out to be repaired—expensive. I bought new tube hoping it would last like the one in 1971. Thought it might work until it corroded. Put in new tube May 22, 1973. Tube was $3.35.

After Charlie Frazier's father came home drunk from the boat club with his son once too often, Mrs. Frazier accompanied them on Saturdays. Mr. Frazier was not happy. I was invited many times, and every time, as we drove across the Flushing Bridge, over its reeking mounds of rusting cars in junkyards below, Mr. Frazier would say to his wife, every time we went over it, without fail, every time, he would say, "Put your shoes on, Frances."

One night Mr. Frazier had the blues so bad he couldn't walk, had to crawl.

What tenacity!

His father: likeable and unlikeable in equal parts.

Jean Shepherd invented Dream Collection Day, where he envisioned everyone taking half-finished model airplanes out of the basement, the half-finished novel, the cracked guitar, the ancient watercolor, and putting them in front of the house. "Everybody will have to do it together—all together," he said. "We'll clean out all these broken, old, sad, poor, wonderful, idiotic, debilitating, defeating dreams."

Dining with Allen Grossman at his favorite restaurant, Villa Pizza of Sienna, I asked him what he was having. "Veal Parmesan," he said. "But I don't recommend it."

One of the main causes of death is fretting about your diet.

To the Editor:

Earlier this year I went to a gay travel show in New York and had a lot of fun. I met a nice lady from Provincetown who told me I should visit. So I sent away for information. I got a pretty cool brochure that made me think it was going to be a summer vacation I'd never forget, and I made a reservation at a small guest house. I got an email message from the Provincetown Business Guild that said it was the gayest place in America. I couldn't wait!

What a crock! The guest house was run by a guy who wanted to have sex with everyone who stayed there. It was disgusting. I hope that is not what growing old in Provincetown is all about.

The bars close at 1 A.M. (which means last call for alcohol is at 12:30).

That's not gay, that's lame.

I went to the gay beach and was told by the ranger to keep my clothes on or I would be arrested.

How gay is that?

The streets are full of straight people, and the town is hardly hip.

Gay? I don't think so.

Don't pretend to be something you're not. Be real and admit the truth. The gayest place in America is not P'town.

Sincerely,
Stan Richwine

Leave the bum speak.

Samuel Kress, the wealthy five-and-ten cents store magnate, bought millions of dollars of art through the dealer, Joseph Duveen. After a lifetime of collecting, he asked Duveen whether his collection was superior to Andrew Mellon's, a Duveen client and rival. Duveen replied, "You have the mountains. Mellon has the peaks."

A liar, but an honest liar.

Frank Sinatra almost drowned in a rip tide in Hawaii while making *None But the Brave*, and the next day he told reporters, "I just got a little water on my bird is all."

The dean asked the new chair of the English Department if he would be interested in annexing the Journalism Department. The new chair replied, "Literature is news that stays news."

OUR LADY OF MOUNT CARMEL ROMAN CATHOLIC CHURCH, EAST BOSTON

GUIDELINES FOR COUNTING THE MONEY

1. Check at the top of the page if there is one or two collections.

2. The flowered bag is always for the church collection. The white bag is always the extra collection.

3. Each bag will have a note in it telling you which collection it is. You will enter the tally into the proper mass on the page. With bills, coins and checks.

4. Empty the offertory bag on the page. Count bills first. Then you can hand count coins. It will never be more than a few dollars. Then the checks. Open the envelopes.

   Put the bills in packs of twenty-five with a thin brown band around them. If there is a check which is not in an envelope, take an extra envelope from the bottom drawer on the left hand side of desk and write the month and Sunday of it. Then write in the name of the check-giver if the amount is more than $5. If $5 or less, forget it.

   After counting the coins, enter bills, coin and checks and total the amount for that mass.

5. Repeat the same for the second collection. But there will be no envelopes in that collection, unless it is

for the Elevator Fund. Then enter tally and add and put down total for that mass.

6. Checks

   There will be a bank tally sheet for checks. Enter them by their number which is normally on the top right of the checks. That is the bank number. It usually runs several digits. Then enter the amount after each check. I think there are 119 entries on a tally sheet. Then add them up and put the amount on the side. When you use a second Bank Tally Sheet mark it II and so on.

7. If any Mass money comes in do not enter this at all on the sheet. All other items, *e.g.*, money for flowers can be entered, or for a gift to the church.

8. When you get four packs of twenty-five singles take bills out of brown wrappers and put them into the blue 100s wrapper. It is easier to handle these.

9. Count big bills indiscriminately, *e.g.*, 5s and 10s and 20s all to make a hundred. Then put them into a brown wrapper.

10. Remember you will find the key for the counting closet up in back of the door. When you are finished, lock up the counting closet door and return the key to its place.

11. You can come in through the church and count at 11 A.M. just after the 10 o'clock mass. You will have on hand bags from the 4 and the 7:30 and 9 and 10:15. You will have completed these by the time the 11:30 bag comes in.

    Enter all figures in pencil on the sheet in case you have to change them with additions.

    If the telephone rings you do not have to answer it.

"*Sleeping Late on Judgment Day* is so singular and alive it couldn't have been written by anyone other than Jane Mayhall."

"Just three notes and you know it's Herb Alpert!"

"This steak speaks for itself!"

From a student literary magazine:

> Colophon. The colophon is a place for us, the designers of this little book, to share with the reader where we found the lovely type and images used between these pages.
>
> It's an opportunity for us to give credit to the illustrator Don Almquist, who will likely never know that his illustrations in *The Country Journal Book of Birding and Bird Attraction in 1981* are the centerpiece for the design of this, our twelfth issue…

At the end of the *Jimmy Durante Show*, Jimmy said good night to the audience and walked across the stage which was dark except for a string of streetlights. He turned off each lamp and, when he reached the final one, he said, "Goodnight, Mrs. Calabash, wherever you are."

> I had love once in the palm of my hand.
> See the lines there.
> How we played
> its game, are playing now…

> Walk On By
> Walk Away Renee

Walk This Way
Walk Don't Run
Walk the Walk
Walk Me Home

On October 10, 2004, as the final mass was being celebrated at Our Lady of Mount Carmel Church in Boston, a statue of the Virgin Mary fell to the ground from its perch in front of the altar.

The retired Victorian professor, when called by a colleague, said he was in touch with the late drummer Elvin Jones's widow. He was meeting with her to try to talk her out of her campaign to have the drums renamed the *jones*.

Night fell inky.

To the College Community:

From: Benjamin Cronin, Property Manager

I am pleased to announce the appointment of Denise Davis to the position of Assistant Property Manager, effective October 1st.

Denise, a three-year veteran of the Property Management Department, has previously served as Property Management Assistant.

No one knew a thing about the forty-five-year-old woman stabbed to death inside her studio apartment on the Upper East Side. Even the police are struggling to learn about the woman, Mandy Malabar Carlyle. She lived alone, and clung fiercely to ritual. Minutes before she was murdered, she followed her Sunday morning routine: from 1729 First Avenue, she walked across the street for a copy of *The New York Times*, dug out $2.40 and counted out the last ten cents in pennies. "Always the last ten cents in pennies," said Abdul Alsolhi at the East Side Grocery. Summer, fall, spring or winter, suede gloves shielded her hands. She wore beige suits and heavy makeup. She had paid $12,000 cash for a year's rent, saying she left California because her home burned down, yet she did not own a house there, but had lived in a seedy residential hotel a block from the Walk of Fame on Hollywood Boulevard. "There are not too many people we have to bury in Potter's Field," Lieutenant Jorge Ramon said. "We're up against the wall. She's a mystery woman."

We see freedom in the flight of a bird, but not in the flight of a fly.

Dear Write to Know:

I am looking for a store that sells canes. The cane I am looking for in particular is one that will bounce up on its own if it is dropped. This would be a great help when a disabled person drops his cane and can't pick it up. Do any readers know the name of the store that sells these canes?

G.C.

I read a biography of Jimmy Durante to learn the identity of Mrs. Calabash. It said that Mrs. Calabash didn't exist and was a name invented by the producers to intrigue the audience.

Chekhov enters without knocking.

William Woodward III, 54, whose society family was known as much for its violent deaths as for its wealth, died Sunday on the Upper East Side of Manhattan after a 14-story plunge from his apartment. No foul play was suspected. Mr. Woodward came from a family haunted by well-publicized deaths.

His mother killed his father, then later killed herself shortly before the publication of a book by Truman Capote that gave a fictionalized account of the father's death. Mr. Woodward's brother killed himself by jumping from a hotel. Mr. Woodward ran twice for office. In 1981, he spent more than $100,000 of his own money during a Democratic primary campaign for an at-large City Council seat from Manhattan. Asked by a reporter what he hoped to bring to the Council, Mr. Woodward pulled out a piece of paper and read, "Boldness, innovativeness, cost-consciousness and independence."

When Byron thinks, he is a child.

She was dying, and he was going to die.

My tenure-track colleague returned to my office and told me he had abandoned *Lives of the Poets for Children* because his daughter cried whenever he read parts to her. His piece on Emily Dickinson ended, "She was buried in a white coffin."

He asked me if I would read something the department might find acceptable, part of a memoir, *Madeline and Me.*

Chapter One

When I was a teenager, my mother's younger sister, Madeline, stayed with us every summer. She has lost her husband years ago in an accident when he drunkenly steered his speedboat under a dock and was decapitated.

I came home from school one afternoon to an empty house, my favorite time, because I could enter the guest room and go through Madeline's things. She was in her forties and my crush on her grew each year. I opened her perfume bottle and inhaled.

On the bed I saw a pair of white panties. I didn't think twice, I just plunged them into my pocket.

On Saturday my mother gathered the clothes from the hampers and stripped the beds. I was in the basement, trying to assemble my grandfather's old wine-making equipment, the wooden device that corked bottles, and the long tubes through which the wine would flow.

When my mother called me, I knew why. I had left Madeline's panties under my pillow.

Upstairs, my mother, red-faced, asked, "Where did you get these?"

"I found them," I said.

"You found them?" She held them between her thumb and forefinger as if they were a repulsive thing, which they were, wrinkled and stained. "Where?"

"I can't remember."

"Are you going through my sister's things?"

"Madeline said I could have them."

She didn't believe me and rushed to get Madeline.

We all sat at the glass-topped table. My mother apologized to Madeline for my conduct, but to my surprise, Madeline lied and said that she saw me with her underwear and told me to keep it. She was flushed, embarrassed and now we were a pair, guilty and guilty.

My mother stared, openmouthed. The panties laid on the table. I was amazed by how soiled they were, and I felt I should have taken better care of them.

"This is unhealthy," my mother said. "Unhealthy," she said. "Tom, you will have to be punished. And Madeline, I'm really shocked and disappointed at your lack of judgment."

My mother got up and went into her bedroom and we heard her dresser drawer open. Madeline kept her eyes on the placemat in front of her. Although she was forty-two, she looked very young at that moment. My mother returned with a riding crop, a braided slender leather strip about sixteen inches long. I had seen it before—I admit to rummaging freely through everyone's clothing. There was a long knife inside the handle.

"I'm going to wean you off this crush you have on Madeline," she said. "Madeline, I want you to move your chair over here." She pointed to a place away from the table, at the entrance to my room. Madeline did what she was told and my mother made her sit.

She said to me, "Lie over your aunt's lap." I developed an instant erection at the thought of pressing myself against Madeline's thighs, and both of them noticed.

I laid across her polka dot dress. My cock bent painfully against her as my hands pressed against the rug. My mother began switching my ass with the crop, but I couldn't feel anything through my jeans, and my lack of response made her swing harder. Although I wasn't moving, she told Madeline to hold me and Madeline pushed her palms against my back.

Frustrated, my mother ordered me up and she unsnapped, unzipped my jeans and pulled them down. My erection bulged against my jockey shorts and she pushed me against Madeline again, though Madeline's dress had pulled up and my cock was rubbing her bare thighs.

The next cuts from the crop stung, and I yelped a few times, but that was nothing compared to the sound I made as I ejaculated. When I finished, it was like the aftershock of an explosion—total silence, a silence in which I heard my loud breathing, as well as my mother's.

I stood up, the front of my underpants visibly wet.

To my shock, my mother yanked down my underpants, and my cock flopped out, slimy and semi-erect. She lifted it toward Madeline and said, "You are responsible for this." She went into the kitchen and came back with a paper towel and wiped me off. Madeline's eyes were wide—a drop of white saliva formed on her lower lip. I began to get hard again.

"Don't you apologize?" she said to Madeline whose face was now bright red.

"And you, what's wrong with you? Pull up your pants."

She reached over, grabbed Madeline by the hand and pulled her into the next room and over the bed. She told me to hold her hands. Madeline moved as if in a trance, making no sound and no resistance. My mother pulled her dress up and her panties down so that her white backside shimmied over the tasseled bedspread. She went into the kitchen and Madeline looked up at me and squeezed my hands. My mother returned with a long black piece of leather, a razor strop belonging to her father that hung in the closet with the broom, feather duster and mop.

She stepped back and swung. The strap hitting Madeline's wide buttocks made a crack that emptied Madeline's lungs of breath. She gasped and ground her head into the bedspread. A wide red slash appeared on her skin. My mother's eyes, which I just noticed were green, blared with purpose and she struck Madeline again and again.

After ten strokes, when Madeline was sobbing into the bedspread and her hands were limp in mine, my mother told me come around and stand next to her.

We stared together at my rumpled aunt, her dress around her waist, her panties around one foot and her sandals on the floor, having been kicked off.

"Shame on you," she said to Madeline. "Shame on you." She went to the bathroom and came back with some hand cream. She squirted it onto her palms and then applied it gently to Madeline's swollen and red buttocks. Very purposefully, she spread my aunt's cheeks apart, and held them that way for a few seconds so that I could see part of the vulva and her crinkled balloon knot of an anus.

A coming of rage story.

A murder suspect was nailed yesterday after cops tracked him through the wristwatch apparently ripped from him by his victim and discovered at the slaying scene. The watch, a digital Timex with a memory, contained the suspect's bank account number. "He had direct deposit," said Lt. Jorge Ramon, commander of the 19th Precinct. "We knew that on the first of the month he'd go to the bank and pick up his money." So detectives staked out the Banco Popular at 161 Livingston St. and nabbed Caesar Vincent-Venezia, 39, when he showed up, charging him with murder, attempted rape and possession of a dangerous weapon in the death of Mandy Malabar Carlyle.

The Group of the Oblong Table consisted of Mel Brooks, Zero Mostel, Joseph Heller and a few other friends who met every Tuesday night at a cheap Chinese restaurant. After one of the party ate all of the meat in a dish, a firm rule was established: For every bite of beef, fish, pork or chicken, you had to have a bite of rice in between.

I met a woman jogger on a trail of the National Seashore during hunting season. She said she had seen a flock of wild turkeys scattering across the road, and her only thought was that they were in danger. She was upset, certain that hunters would find them. I was sure her story would end with a bloody description of wounded or dead birds, but she said, obviously grieved, that soon after seeing the turkeys, she passed two hunters, and something—she didn't know what—prompted her to shout as she ran by, "There's turkeys back there!"

I'll be gone, you'll be gone, we'll all be gone.

A metal sign on the fire escape of my childhood apartment in Jackson Heights, New York City said: Do Not Sit on Fire Escape. Five Dollar Fine for Removing This Sign.

Sculptor Richard Rosenblum amassed the finest collection of Chinese scholar's rocks in the world. On a trip to China in 1987, he visited a garden that held beautiful examples, and workers there tried to sell them to him, but each time the deal was about to be made, they demurred to the next highest official. After a frustrating hour, he insisted on seeing the owner. An old man appeared and told him the rocks were never for sale, but that the workers were grateful for the opportunity to practice capitalism.

A second biography of Jimmy Durante said that Mrs. Calabash was a waitress in a Calabash, North Carolina, diner who Jimmy fell in love with on a tour.

Dear Professor:

Thank you again for the letter of recommendation. I was accepted into Jeju National University but found the school was not up to my expectations and I decided to unroll.

There were many reasons, some far worse than the troubles that sent me into philosophy. The smallest was a vibrant attack on a vending machine attributed to me but of which I am innocent. Hooligans urinated into the coin slot, dousing the money. I wasn't even nearby, but I was blamed.

After some time alone, I decided to apply to Utrecht University, in the Netherlands.

I ask you, if you could once again send a letter of recommendation. I will send a form that the Utrecht University requires.

Your former student,
Bertrand

God tempers the wind to the shorn lamb.

In 1963, President John Kennedy gave a speech in Berlin, and to show his solidarity with the people of that city and, in opposition to the building of the Berlin wall, he proclaimed, *"Ich bin ein Berliner,"* meaning, *I am a Berliner.*

According to Hugh Mulligan, the Associated Press reporter covering the story, what JFK really said was, *I am a Jelly Donut,* as the Berliner pastry is known in parts of Germany.

Pasta is a matter of seconds. Baseball and sex are games of inches.

Our daughter's eighth grade teacher, Mrs. Niles, invited us to a party. She introduced us to her husband, a minister. I asked where he preached and he said he was currently without a church. Another guest was a disc jockey, but he had lost his job when the radio station had changed from country to talk. A third person planned to open a pet store, acquired some inventory, and was searching for a location. He had recently sold a tarantula to Mr. and Mrs. Niles. We stared at it creeping around the terrarium. The minister reached in, grabbed it and let it walk up his arm. He offered it to me, but I said it would be dangerous. He said that no, it had been de-nectared. Every creature in that house had lost its place in the world.

An ex-convict was found guilty of murder yesterday in the stabbing death of a woman in her Upper East Side apartment in 1995. A jury in State Supreme Court in Manhattan convicted Caesar Vincent-Venezia, 39, of the murder of Mandy Malabar Carlyle, 45, who was stabbed 14 times in the neck and chest during a robbery in her apartment. Jurors said outside the court that they believed Mr. Vincent-Venezia knew what he was doing when he killed Ms. Carlyle, who neighbors said had lived a solitary existence. Mr. Vincent-Venezia's lawyer, John Iannuzzi, said during the trial that his client was delusional, claiming descent from Napoleon III and that he killed the woman as a human sacrifice because she got too close to his throne.

A man's hatred is always concentrated on the thing that makes him conscious of his bad qualities.

Christ's utter failure came at the Crucifixion in the tragic words, "My God, my God, why hast thou forsaken me?" Christ saw that his whole life, devoted to the truth according to his best conviction, had been a terrible illusion. On the cross, his mission deserted him. But because he had lived so fully and devotedly he won through to the Resurrection body.

We all must do just what Christ did. We must make our experiment. We must make mistakes. We must live out our own vision of life. And there will be error. If you avoid error, you do not live. In a sense it may be said that every life is a mistake, for no one has found the truth.

Primo Levi was asked when he wrote *Survival in Auschwitz*. He said, "On Sunday afternoons. And not every Sunday afternoon."

Ancient Brother LaSalle taught typing. Students sat behind a different machine each day: sometimes a Smith-Corona, sometimes an IBM. Everyone liked the tall Royals best because they were perfect for folding your arms across and resting your head. But whenever a student fell asleep, LaSalle yelled, "Float!" meaning the student had to leave and walk the halls for the rest of the period, in danger of being smacked by the roving assistant principal. If the student slouched on his way out, LaSalle ordered him to "Walk like an American!" One afternoon we came to class to find him asleep at his desk. Someone whispered another of his favorite phrases, "*Note Bene!*" into his ear, but he did not wake up, he had floated off the earth.

My father used to sing, "Fly me to the moon. And leave me on the moon."

Humphrey Bogart attended a formal dinner party where the guest of honor was the Italian Ambassador. The host asked Bogart to refrain from his usual foul language at the table. Bogart was on his best behavior; he didn't say a word. At the end of the evening, when the ambassador took leave of each guest. Bogart said, "You speak very good English."

"Thank you," the ambassador said. "I had an English governess."

"Did you fuck her?" Bogart asked.

Above comparison.

In 1953, the psychiatrist Renatus Hartogs interviewed Lee Harvey Oswald when he was thirteen due to truancy from school. His report stated:

> He likes to give the impression that he doesn't care about others and rather likes to keep to himself so that he is not bothered and does not have to make the effort of communicating. It was difficult to penetrate the emotional wall behind which this boy hides and he provided us with sufficient clues, permitting us to see intense anxiety, shyness, feelings of awkwardness and insecurity as the main reasons for his

withdrawal tendencies and solitary habits. Lee told us: "I don't want a friend and I don't like to talk to people." Lee has a vivid fantasy life, turning around the topics of omnipotence and power, through which he tries to compensate for his present shortcomings and frustrations. He did not enjoy being together with other children and when we asked him whether he prefers the company of boys to [that] of girls he answered, "I dislike everybody."

In 1969, Renatus Hartogs helped many of my fellow college students avoid the draft. After a short interview in his Manhattan office, he wrote a letter concluding they were inclined toward violence, child-molesting or drug abuse. Little by little, his letters were turned away. Word came they were no longer accepted at the White-hall Street draft board, but still worked in New Haven. I forgot about him until years later, in a girl's apartment in Iowa City, where I browsed through *Cosmopolitan* and saw he had a sex advice column. And soon after that I read about his being sued by a female patient:

> *Hartogs treated Julie Roy from 1969 - '70 with sex. The plaintiff said she was emotionally injured. Dr. Hartogs said there was no law against seduction. The Court awarded both Compensatory & Puni-tive damages. Appeals Court affirmed, said this was malpractice, not seduction, but dropped punitive damages, because, they said, he was incompetent, not malicious. Dr. Hartogs sued his insurance com-pany, who said treatment with sex was not covered under professional Rx, was not "treatment," and*

they won. The case was made into a book & movie;
Dr. Hartogs received no royalties.

I hated to read when I was a boy. My mother brought me books about the Hardy Boys, who were always seeking treasure in caves or discovering old cabins full of mysteries. Living in a railroad flat in Queens, I couldn't relate to these tales, greatly disappointing my mother. One day she came home with a hardcover book she bought at Woolworth's, its shiny cover featuring a color drawing of Matt Dillon of the TV series *Gunsmoke*. I read it right through, hoping to please her, and when I finished, I walked into the kitchen and said, "Thanks, Mom. That was the best book I ever read!"

She looked up at me from the tomato sauce she was ladling onto English muffins to make pizzas, and said, "And you are the stupidest boy I ever met."

Why no meow?

The dean returned from a trip to the Inca Trail, and told the department chairs of her experience, describing with great excitement the beautiful thatched huts, which she sometimes called thutched hats.

No comparison.

Are certain words inherently poetic, like *azure* and *gaze*?

During a vile squabble with the dean, my colleague said how he wished he were famous, to be so valued by the administration for having won major prizes that he could walk into the president's office and threaten to resign if the situation with the dean was not resolved in his favor. It did not occur to him to wish to be so famous that he could simply quit and not have to think about the situation at all. He desired celebrity more than freedom.

It's a hard birth, a short life and death forever, so why work?

John Cage gave a performance at The New School, part of which involved releasing handfuls of sand onto the stage, the thin sound of which had the audience totally enraptured. At the question and answer session afterward, someone asked in a reverential tone where he got the sand, speculating Tibet or Burma. Cage said, "From the ashtray in the lobby."

In 1811 Stendhal visited Florence and spent hours in front of Michelangelo's *David*, Botticelli's *Primavera* and Giotto's frescoes, causing him to faint. In 1979, a Florentine psychiatrist said he had noted a hundred cases of the same dizziness and nausea, and labeled it Stendhal's Syndrome, a condition brought on by an over-exposure to the city's art treasures.

I bumped into Michael Mazur on his way to life drawing class and I asked him where were his materials. He pulled a yellow stub from his pocket and said, "Number two pencil."

The college announced the hiring of a new head of IT, Hari Nair. But the press release misspelled his name. It asked us to welcome Hair Nair.

Five years later, when he moved on, we were invited to his goodbye party and the same mistake was made on the invitation. He arrived as Hair Nair and left as Hair Nair.

> I could not die — with You —
> For One must wait
> To shut the Other's Gaze down —

Overweight heavyweight prizefighter Buster Mathis, who weighed 256 pounds, fought Muhammad Ali in 1971 in a match billed as "The Mountain Comes to Muhammad."

At the meeting to decide what courses might be offered in the new Institute of Liberal Arts, the dean said the center would give instructors the chance to teach areas of specialty outside of their fields.

"For instance," she said, "I could teach a course in North Dakota humor."

Someone said, "You've got me laughing."

Beyond comparison.

The Order of the Occult Hand replaced the Defective Busbar Club, open to any journalist who used those words in a story, such as, "Officials attributed the cause of the fire to a defective busbar."

The most personal section of Italo Calvino's *Hermit in Paris: Autobiographical Writings,* is its first half, the diary that Calvino kept during his visit to the United States in 1959, when he was 36. This material, published for the first time, shows Calvino as a wide-eyed explorer who is struck by American culture, including TV dinners, Broadway premieres and the weight of the Sunday *New York Times,* "a bundle of paper you can hardly carry in your two arms." He describes horseback riding in Central Park, and the dilemma of arriving in New Orleans for Mardi Gras without having booked a room in advance. He is amused at the size of American sedans, commenting that "even the taxis have really long tailfins." It is as if an occult hand placed Calvino in our country so we could appreciate our own eccentricities.

Don't drop your guard.

The psychiatrist said that the TV show *Leave It to Beaver* was a big hit in the late fifties/early sixties because it was subconsciously sexual. The star's name was Beaver Cleaver. The first name, he said, was slang for the vulva, and the second very close to cleavage.

> With more than admiration he admired
> Her azure veins, her alabaster skin,
> Her coral lips, her snow-white dimpled chin.

Life and art: the bull and the bullfighter.

His poems seemed the product of a thorny man of the study, written with a thorn.

The new dean was introduced as someone who would humanize the sciences and simonize the humanities.

Bidding farewell to lyricism to succumb to the vulgarity of narrative.

Alec Guinness plays the roguish artist Gulley Jimson, in *The Horse's Mouth*. In one scene, he's teaching a class of wealthy women to paint. Each dowager stands behind her easel, painting a quaint and traditional landscape. One woman has drawn a few squiggly black lines across a white cloud. Jimson approaches her easel, points with great consternation to that part of the painting and says, "A little chancy, don't you think?"

The first man who had nothing drew a circle around it.

In grammar school, when our homework was to write sentences using particular vocabulary words, I did the assignments twice. Once, the correct way, and again for my friends' amusement. The latter included: "I *plum* forgot it" and "We had a *suggestion* at our house."

In college, I read there are two kinds of thinkers: convergent and divergent. The first reasons conventionally, and does well; the second lands off the beaten path. I was the second, wearing the mask of the first.

And now I wonder, has that mask stuck?

Spare a nickel for an old altar boy, Father?

Man is needed to illuminate the obscurity of the Creator.

Massacre, Marksman, Luger and John.

I tried on a sport coat at a men's shop. A salesman approached and said, "It fits perfectly." I continued to look in the mirror.

"It fits perfectly," he said again. "Shall I wrap it up?"

It did fit well, but something was off.

I said, "You're right. It fits perfectly, but I don't like it."

Some people need ideas which can be expressed only in words.

Though the events in this book bear similarity to those of that long malaise, my life, many of the characters and happenings are creations solely of the imagination.

Tell a story twice, it's fiction.

Charlie's father said to a blind man near the subway, "Hey, blind man, tell me what you see."

It was a fatal New Year's Day in New York City for ten New Yorkers and a French tourist—victims of stabbings, muggings, shootings and other crimes.

Police made thirty-four arrests in the Times Square area—including five for grand larceny and assault—and filed sixty-seven other reports in what they described as a "mild" New Year's Eve.

A twenty-year-old woman was thrown to her death from a Times Square hotel, blocks from where 300,000 revelers had gathered hours before to mark the New Year.

Police found the unidentified woman's partially clothed body at 5:40 A.M. near the Carter Hotel. Her hands were tied behind her back.

Meanwhile, James Jones, 25, was arrested and charged with stabbing his brother, Mamon Jones, 27, with scissors yesterday morning after an argument in Mamon's Brook Avenue apartment.

In Brooklyn, an elderly woman was found strangled, an unidentified man was found shot in the head and two unidentified people were stabbed to death.

Francisco Moreno, 33, of 60th Street, Sunset Park, Brooklyn, was stabbed to death by his brother-in-law after the two argued in front of the victim's home, police said.

Two hours earlier, a thirty-four-year-old man was found dead on the sidewalk at Himrod St. and Evergreen Avenue, Brooklyn, with a hunting knife in his back.

Elsewhere in the city, Andre Stubbin, 18, was shot dead in Harlem when he refused to hand over his coat to an assailant.

Police are questioning Henry Yorio, 69, in the 8 A.M. Brooklyn strangling of his sixty-two-year-old wife, Helen. He was hospitalized for treatment of hypertension after his wife's death.

Memories are hunting horns whose sound dies on the wind.

Delacroix: He had a sun in his head and storms in his heart.

Ida suffered from trichotillomania, pulling her hair out. Her psychiatrist told her to go to Chinatown and buy a fresh chicken, and when she felt the urge to hurt herself, she should pluck the feathers instead. She went to Kneeland Street in Boston, to a place with a sign that read LIVE CHICKENS/FRESH KILLED. When her turn came, Ida told the clerk she wanted one chicken and paid for it. She moved down the line, where another man held up her bird and she nodded. Then he tossed it into what she didn't know was a centrifugal tumbling machine that removed all the feathers. He threw it into a plastic bag and she was ushered out the door.

In 2003, Stanley Kunitz was dying for the first time. He laid in bed in his 12th Street apartment, surrounded by friends, mostly women. My wife, in town to give a reading at the New School, visited him to say goodbye. At the end of their talk, Stanley said that he had something important for her to tell me. She told me this story on her return, and I couldn't imagine what this could be. He said to tell me that "the best thing I'd ever done…" and here I waited for his judgment on my career or my work… "Tell John," he said, "that the best thing he ever did, was to marry you."

Stanley recovered a few days later, rising from his bed and ordering three more years of batteries for his hearing aid, exactly the number of years he would live after this first death at 97.

When you fall in love, keep a little bit of your heart for yourself.

The philosophy professor said that the phrase *It is what it is* "yields no enlightenment on a subject. It says nothing but *a* equals *a*."

Almost every boy in my neighborhood in Queens joined the Boy Scouts or the Sea Cadets. On Friday nights, they put on uniforms and gathered in church basements or Masonic lodges. I had no interest in either group, but one Friday, my friend Jimmy, a scout, invited me along. All the boys wore brown uniforms with gold kerchiefs at the neck. They compared patches and medals. The scoutmaster, Mr. McCarthy, welcomed me warmly and I joined a crew building a go-cart.

I held a vice grips on a bolt but slipped and sliced the web of skin between my thumb and forefinger.

Mr. McCarthy remained calm, grabbed my wrist and led me to the stage where he called for a white box marked with a red X. He splashed the cut with peroxide, swabbed it with Unguentine, dabbed it with iodine and Mercurochrome, and slathered it with every salve and ointment in his first aid kit. The whole time, he displayed each product and held it aloft to the room, explaining its medicinal properties. He unrolled a skein of gauze, and wrapped my forearm, working his way to my wrist and then toward the wound and past it until he had covered all of my fingers. Then he took an Ace bandage and did the same. When he finished, he held my hand high, as if I had won a boxing match.

On the way home, Jimmy asked me how I liked the meeting, and I said Mr. McCarthy was a great guy. Jimmy asked to look at my hand, and I showed it to him under a streetlight. It was twice the size due to the heavy bandaging. We admired the little steel, crab-like clips that held the end of the bandage in place. As we peered at Mr. McCarthy's work, we simultaneously saw, in the place between my thumb and forefinger, the bloody gash, surrounded by banks of gauze and bandage, clearly accessible.

Joseph Butler (1692–1752) was an English bishop, theologian and philosopher known for his critique of Thomas Hobbes's egoism and John Locke's theory of personal identity. Butler influenced many philosophers, including David Hume and Adam Smith.

His most remembered epigram is: *Every thing is what it is, and not another thing.*

Roast Turkey: Take a big fat bird, shove it full of popcorn, throw it in the oven, turn it up to 500, and when the popcorn pops and shoots the turkey's ass off, it's cooked.

During the past week—from Monday, December 26 to Sunday, January 1, the members of the Truro Police Department logged fifty-five calls. Of those calls, there were four fire/rescue calls, twenty-five traffic stops resulting in six violations, suspicious activity and a found violin.

Making love has a beginning, a middle and an end, but not necessarily in that order.

In 1958, Isaiah Berlin wrote in his essay, "Two Concepts of Liberty," *Everything is what it is…*

A stingy and mean widow, Mrs. Simpson, lived across the parking lot from the arts center where I worked. Our janitor, Ed, had to handle her complaints: lights too bright, cars parked too close to her house, rose bushes brushing her car as she pulled into her driveway. She never had any visitors, but suddenly the same man arrived daily. A few weeks later he seemed to be living there. I mentioned this to Ed who said the man was a friend of his, a widower, who had told him months earlier, "I wish I could put my Social Security check together with hers." Ed told me they had married, adding, "And now he wishes he was never born."

For bitter, or for worse.

The poets in the MFA program gave brilliant lectures that inspired students to look deeply into how great poems were made. But one student came to my office, upset, pointing out that when these same faculty members read their own poems, the drop off from the height of the critical intelligence to the almost ordinary creative work was apparent and he found it paradoxical. He said since the whole point of the lecture was to help the student poets in the audience write better, to understand how serious art is made—how can that happen if the authors of those insights were unable to apply them to their own work? So, he asked, what was to be gained from these lectures?

Learning is not the accumulation of knowledge, but the application of knowledge.

There is no mystery in art. Do the things you can see and they will show you what you cannot see.

Proust left a hotel and asked the doorman to call him a coach. The coach arrived, and Proust went through his pockets for a tip but found no change. He said to the doorman, "Excuse me, may I borrow two francs?"

"Of course, Monsieur Proust," the doorman said.

Proust thought for a moment and said, "Oh never mind. Keep them. They were for you."

A wealthy trustee of the college, Nettie Budinger, threw a bash for the board at her mansion. Over cocktails in the living room, each department chair took turns touting faculty accomplishments. Drinks flowed for two hours and then Mrs. Budinger thanked the speakers and described the college's strategic plan, which included recruiting more students from diverse backgrounds. The last item caused her to look toward the kitchen where she praised the work of our lone international student, Iranga, who was preparing a Sri Lankan feast for the guests. She called his name, but he did not appear. She called again, and again, and finally he emerged from the kitchen, wearing only a pair of shorts, hair stuck to his head, dripping sweat, arms at his sides, having been cooking since morning.

"Iranga," she asked. "How long have you been here?"

He said with great feeling, "Too long!"

America is a nation difficult to judge. There is no precedent for it in history.

Bad is as bad does.

The professor's play, which he wrote on a Fulbright to Nigeria, began with the words, "Bwana, there a body in the road."

These are the schnitzels.

I like the country. It is a nice spot.

The poet David Ignatow wrote about working as a hospital receptionist when Zero Mostel approached the desk to inquire about his mother's condition:

> It was my job to tell you she was dead.
> I had read of you, a great clown
> in off-Broadway productions.
> I wanted to make known to you my admiration.
> You were pathetic as the son of a dead woman,
> a mother's tolerance of your faults was gone.

Nearly two dozen of Bashir's paintings had been in the permanent collection of the Saddam Arts Center, Baghdad's national gallery, which had been trashed and vandalized. Bashir became very depressed when he saw they had been slashed to ribbons, but he said, "I have trained myself not to be sad, because everything in life is temporary."

The August block party in Elmhurst meant to bring neighbors together. Lasagna, roast chickens, apple pies and cookies brimmed from card tables set up in front of the attached railroad flats. Families sat in folding chairs by the curb, wearing crazy hats and Hawaiian shirts. Bottles of wine and coolers of beer rested under the seats. Soon ethnic slurs were heard, followed by a knife fight. Tony Devitch, a steamfitter, slashed Jimmy Donlon, the florist's delivery boy, with a switchblade, bloodying his turquoise muscle shirt. Jimmy whipped his thick garrison belt around Tony's throat. More knives snapped open, followed by lunging and side-stepping until patrol cars arrived. Some of the belligerents ran away but those who stayed focused on the black asphalt, where, illuminated by a streetlight, there was a length of yellow intestine tinged with pink. The knife fighters surrounded it, sympathetically touching their abdomens, wondering who had been disemboweled in the fracas, who might had drifted off with such an injury, when a little girl ran over and picked it up: a section of an Hawaiian lei.

> I was feelin' so bad
> I asked my family doctor just what I had
> I said, "Doctor!"
> (Doctor!)
> "Mr. M.D!"
> (Doctor!)
> "Can you tell me
> What's ailin' me?"
> (Doctor!)
> He said, "Yeah, yeah, yeah, yeah, yeah!"
> (Yeah, yeah, yeah, yeah, yeah!)

Oscar Wilde's friends came to the inn to take him to lunch and heard a commotion of moans and rustling clothes behind his door. Wilde finally yelled, "Just a minute. I'm almost finished with this page."

A *Boston Globe* reporter was fired for quoting people she had invented. They did not exist, but exemplified a point of view she wanted to register. How different is that from her going out and interviewing people until she found someone with the opinion she sought and quoting him?

Anglophone. Francophone. We'll-all-be-phone.

My son's goldfish died, and I told him that eventually everything dies, that everything breaks, including toys, computers, cars and that he shouldn't be sad about it because everything in life is temporary. He took this very well. A few weeks later, his friend visited and, during their game of racing cars, the boy's convertible lost a wheel and he began to cry. My son ran up to me, cupped his hand to his mouth, and whispered, "He doesn't know!"

Ray Carver, talking about a raucous binge with his friends, would say, "That was a real pea-roller!" His red face would smile at the memory. I can still hear him say it today. "A real pea-roller."

The Queen of Sheba is only for a magic kind of love, never for matrimony. If you were to marry her, you would both be destroyed and your soul would disintegrate.

In the mid-sixties, a girl in my neighborhood loved the song, "She's About a Mover," by the Sir Douglas Quintet.

This was during the English invasion, featuring the Beatles, the Dave Clark Five and Herman's Hermits. She wrote to the Sir Douglas fan club and received information. When I asked her about it, I found her opinion had changed. She was disgusted. "They're not English," she said. "They're from Texas, and some of them are Mexican!" They had taken the name in fun and cashed in on the trend.

He said his favorite figure in the bible was Ish Kabibble.

A fly landed on the page. We will both disappear, one more slowly than the other.

We bought a strange-looking doll at a crafts fair in Salem and named it Mirabelle. When we showed it to our little daughter, she burst into tears. Worse, the doll was haunted. In a rented house in Provincetown, we heard footsteps in the floor above, a floor closed off in winter to save heat. My wife climbed the steep stairs, flipped open the trap door, and went down the hall to look around. I followed and, as I reached the top step, the door rose and slammed me on the head, almost knocking me out. Nothing was there except for some old boxes, one of which contained Mirabelle. My wife brought her downstairs and the footfalls ended.

As a child, I found the word *wraith* in my father's *Abbott's Pocket Dictionary*, and took it as proof that ghosts existed.

The last sentence of the breakup letter said, "Our tomorrow was yesterday."

100

To the Editor:

There has been a serious misunderstanding regarding events at the fire at Army & Navy Surplus. After the fire, we were asked by one of the detectives if we gave permission to anyone to take statues from our store. We said, "No," statues to us being articles on the top shelf for decoration, not for sale, like the big lady in the corner, the dancers, the weight lifter, the Presidential busts and the standing gold cherubs with candlesticks.

My son Ed went through the store with a fireman and, upon opening the doors to let out the dense smoke, some little wooden fishermen floated out. Three firemen told me that when they used the hose some of these little wooden fishermen drifted onto the street. I said, "Keep them, they're of no importance!"

The last thing on your mind is a small wooden fisherman when your business is burning and your son has an air pack on to save it.

The next day a fireman stopped in to say he had taped one of the little fishermen to the fire truck.

A detective came around and asked if we had given permission to take statues. I never thought of the little wooden fishermen of no consequence that had floated out the front door. Now the detectives contend I changed my story, which is absolutely not so.

The DA called me and I believe the charges against the firemen will be dropped.

We will always be grateful to the Provincetown Fire Department and the other Cape fire departments who came to assist, and put the fire out.

Sincerely,
Mike Walker

Jung tried to establish a dialogue between the individual and the universe without destroying the idea of personality or the ego.

A criminal lawyer told me when his defendant is called to the stand, and he wants sympathy for him, he buys him a shirt two sizes too big, so it appears he has lost weight. When he wants a sickly defendant to appear fit, he buys him a shirt two sizes too small.

Dear Mr. Mailer,

I regret not speaking to you at Renate's party last September. I had a nice talk with Norris, my old tennis pupil, who never liked the sun because she preferred to be that beautiful color, "fish-belly white."

The fact that you didn't slug me makes me think you are mellowing.

Yours,
Anonymous

The reward of art is not fame or success, but intoxication: that is why so many bad artists are unable to give it up.

The obituary of Skip Spence, psychedelic musician and founding member of both Jefferson Airplane and Moby Grape, who was born on April 18, 1946, appeared in the *New York Times* on April 18, 1999. Phrases in the piece include "institutionalized for many years," "under-age girls," "increasing amounts of hallucinogens," and "went after band members with a fire ax."

A mother's tolerance of his faults was gone.

If the faculty were asked to choose between two doors, one that led to Paradise and the other to a lecture on Paradise, most would choose the lecture.

Heavy in appearance, but light as a cork.

Joyce Franklin, wife of the sculptor, Gil Franklin, gave a dinner party for a group of artists and writers. One of them asked her what she did. "Nothing!" she said. "I do nothing!" The artists and writers repeated this answer for years, over and over, struck by her courage, the courage to do nothing, a courage that Marguerite Duras confessed she lacked when she said, "If I had the courage to do nothing, I'd do nothing. It's because I don't have the courage to do nothing that I write. There is no other reason."

Her canvasses hold colors that caress, an often dusky palette that invites the pupils to relax, to pull close the waning light, to seek the point beyond the horizon. It would be too easy to call a piece like *Two Boats* a seascape. It is infinity. It is a silent, poetic, unrelenting pause in cacophony. It evokes immeasurable loneliness and melancholy, euphoric emptiness and emancipation. It is abstracted isolation in search of togetherness and togetherness in search of isolation. Stepping inside this painting, one—simply—is. This painter's universe, in its large canvasses and expansive horizons, its ghostly, spare shapes, its taut shrouds of opaque atmospheres, is the land of the human condition.

The world is full of objects, more or less interesting. I do not wish to add any more. I prefer simply to state the existence of things in terms of time and place.

It rains on the just and the unjust.

But the just get wetter because the unjust have stolen the just's umbrella.

I remember driving around in my red '59 Impala convertible with the cat's-eye taillights, listening to the song "Popsicles and Icicles" by the Murmaids, with my then favorite gal sitting practically on top of me. No bucket seats, seat belts or big brother government watching, just living and enjoying life. Too bad today's generation will never know that feeling, or anything even close...

Dear Professor:

Thank you! I am so honored you will help me once again.

I have included instructions for letters of recommendation for Utrecht University. I am extremely excited to return to the Netherlands to study philosophy. I plan to continue my studies and earn a Ph.D. as well.

Your former student,
Bertrand

During Sargent Shriver's campaign for president, his staff took him to a bar frequented by sawmill workers at the end of a shift. His campaign manager told him to introduce himself and then buy a beer for the room. He said, "I'd like to buy everyone a beer," and a cheer went up. Then, looking at the bartender, he said, "And I'll have a Chivas on the rocks."

> I wandered in a nightmare
> All around Great Windsor Park,
> And what did you think I found there
> As I stumbled in the dark?
> It was an apple half-bitten,
> And sweetest of all things,
> Five baby teeth had written
> Of the Captains and the Kings.

At one time, all bars were cigar bars.

On the *Tonight Show*, Johnny Carson played Carnac the Magnificent, a mystic who would be told an answer and then would have to guess the question. One night the answer was Yasser Arafat.

The question he read aloud when he opened the envelope was: What is the sound of Dolly Parton taking off her bra?

The letter *o* on the neon sign of the storage company blew out, and the sign read
ST RAGE.

If it wasn't for Goliath, David would be just another shepherd boy.

The tenor saxophone player, Eddie Harris, invented the saxobone, which was a sax with a trombone mouthpiece, and the guitorgan, which fused a guitar and an organ.

Our class praised the student's poem about a robin. At the end of the critique, when it was the poet's turn to respond, he said that the robin was a symbol of capitalism and that he was disappointed in us for not making that connection. He said he couldn't believe how naïve we were about political poetry, as the robin, for him, has always been associated with the wealth of the United States. He said he was disappointed in us as readers, his temper rising. He called us bourgeois, ill-informed, misguided and apathetic. He wondered why he even bothered to bring his poem to a class of such ignoramuses. We wondered what to say, and turned to our teacher, who said, "Poetry allows a success for everyone at the limits of the autonomy of the will, to enact its purposes by other means." He paused. "But I'm afraid this poem doesn't do that."

As Joseph Brodsky and Jonathan Aaron were leaving a restaurant in New York after dinner, the owner stood outside and asked how everything was.

Brodsky said, "Worse than last time."

I'm not sure if you remember me, but I was a student of yours at Emerson (class of '99). You may recall that I was the young woman who got you in trouble with a Boston judge for trying to get me out of jury duty. I still remember how mortified I was, but how your eyes danced at the excitement.

If it wasn't for David, Goliath would be just another bullying giant.

The human race, to which so many of my readers belong...

Kingman Brewster, the president of Yale University, summoned his assistant, Ben Holden, to his office.

"Look out the window," the president said from behind his desk.

In the middle of the courtyard, students surrounded an object made by a visiting sculptor. A fifty-foot pink penis.

"You take care of it," Brewster told Ben, and went back to his paperwork.

I called the retired Victorian specialist. He said he was rinsing broccoli rabe for his flock of canaries—he had turned one of his porches into an aviary.

The Essential Skeeter Davis.

I bought a mechanical pencil on a cold winter night from a huckster on 42nd Street who stood behind a tiny TV tray, held the pencil aloft, and pointing to the lead at its tip, said, "It propels, expels and it misspells, but that's okay, there's an eraser on the other end."

Joe Mac's seaside restaurant serves enormous slabs of prime rib, and if you order it, every person who passes your table will make the same gesture to his companion. Each passerby, male or female, comments silently on the thickness by holding their index finger and thumb apart.

Said, "Doctor, ain't there nothin' I can take?"
I said, "Doctor, to relieve this belly ache,"
I said, "Doctor, ain't there nothin' I can take?"

A fifty-year-old gravedigger married a twenty-five-year-old woman, a woman the age of his daughter. Tired of answering the same question of how they met, he said that he met her in the hospital when his daughter was born.

"I saw the two of them in the nursery," he told people, "and I said to myself I'm gonna raise this one, and marry that one."

Survived by his wife.

They used to call her Mary, and now they call her Ma.

An autobiography has a beginning, a middle and an end, but not necessarily in that order.

Jean Shepherd tells of his long struggle as a kid to acquire a decoder ring offered by the makers of Ovaltine. When he finally gets it in the mail, he nervously and anxiously translates his first secret message, which turns out to be: BE SURE TO DRINK MORE OVALTINE.

Harold von Braunhut invented X-ray glasses (which gave the wearer the ability to see through clothing) and invisible goldfish which came guaranteed that the buyer would never see them. His big hit was Sea Monkeys, brine shrimp, which he claimed could die and be resurrected, as well as trained and hypnotized. He was a member of the Ku Klux Klan and the Aryan Nations.

The famed Rainbow Room was closed by the Cipriani family in 1998 who turned it into a banquet hall. The Hotel, Restaurant & Club Employees Union took out an ad in *The New York Times* in the form of a menu.

SALAD
Hearts of Lettuce

Sorry, the Ciprianis don't serve hearts of lettuce. But a lot of people think the Ciprianis have Hearts of Stone. At a job fair, a representative from Cipriani International refused to interview any Rainbow employees who were union members. All 250 union employees lost their jobs two days before Christmas.

MAIN COURSE
Sirloin Tips

Or is it "Purloin Tips"? The Ciprionis call their banquet waiters "independent contractors." This allows them to avoid paying their share of the employees' Social Security taxes and other obligations. They pay their waiters a flat hourly rate. The waiters do not receive tips. If the banquet waiters do not receive tips, who is getting the service charges placed on the check? Guess. Not a bad haul for restaurateurs who charge $12 for a bottle of water.

SOUP
Cream of Asparagus

Some would call it Cream of Arrogance. Last year, Giuseppe Cipriani told the *Times* that service at the Rainbow Room was a disaster. But the union workers made it the second highest grossing restaurant in the country, ranking only behind Tavern on the Green.

Dessert
Peach Cobbler

Peach Snobbler might be more appropriate. The Ciprianis have treated New York's best food critics almost as badly as they have treated their workers. The *Times'* Bryan Miller was ejected from one restaurant by Giuseppi Cipriani. And Arrigo Cipriani wrote an angry, vindictive letter published in *New York* magazine, saying that food critic Gael Greene and her dinner companions were dressed like eccentric clowns. He even said that Ms. Greene should remove the condom from her tongue.

While there is a lower class, I am in it, and while there is a criminal element, I am of it, and while there is a soul in prison, I am not free.

The first sentence of Mickey Spillane's first book, *I, the Jury*: "I shook the rain from my hat and walked into the room."

A one-way ticket to Palookaville.

I sat next to my friend, the cemetery groundskeeper, during our sons' little league games. One evening he was silent so I asked him if anything was wrong.

He said, "It can get to you, John, cutting the grass over your sister's grave."

Whenever young poets asked to visit Stanley Kunitz, to show him their new work, he always obliged, but said he wanted their poems to do one thing, and gave them this simple yet terrifying standard: *Surprise me.*

M. F. K. Fisher advises buying liquor by the case because it is always discounted by ten per cent. Yet she warns the liquor tends to disappear ten percent more quickly.

One fall day in Provincetown Mike Mazur and I were walking through his garden and it was rainy and windy and we were getting slapped by the stems and branches. Mike said, "With fronds like these, who needs anemones!"

My colleague received a call for help in the middle of the night from his elderly father who lived alone and had fallen. When he arrived, he found his father sitting on the bed, his scalp split and his face a mask of blood. My friend drove him to the emergency room where they waited hours for his cut to be stitched. He took his father home and returned to his house at 2 A.M. He was so agitated that he drank a bottle of wine and went to bed at dawn. He had an early class the next day and he told me he couldn't see think or see straight. He mispronounced words when reciting several poems, and the class lost patience. Toward the end of the session, he misread *pity* as *piety*, and he said the whole class yelled back at him, "*Pity! It's pity!*"

Sculpture: What you knock into when you step back to better see a painting.

I've often mistaken a dog for being human, but never a cat.

I was proud of the way I had planned to introduce Boris Pasternak to my class. I began, "Everyone knows *Dr. Zhivago* from the film made of Boris Pasternak's novel, everyone, that is, except for Yogi Berra. Yogi came home one evening to an empty house. When his wife and son arrived an hour later, Yogi asked where they had been.

'I took Dale to see Dr. Zhivago,' his wife said.

Yogi said, 'What's wrong with him now?'"

When nobody laughed, I realized the students knew neither the author, the novel, the film nor the Yankee catcher.

Sister Grace Winifred, the nun who taught my third grade class, asked for volunteers to take plants home over the Christmas vacation and care for them while the school was closed. I volunteered and, at the end of the day, I selected a potted geranium, carried it in my left hand and then grasped the handles of both my lunch box and school bag in the other. A fight in the cloakroom distracted me, a big pile-up of boys, and I ran in to watch just as a boy yelled, "Someone is stepping on my head!" Sister Grace arrived and threw the boys back into the classroom. I went to my desk and picked up the plant. I grabbed the handle of my schoolbag. The lunchbox was on the floor. Although I had done it before, now I couldn't figure out how I managed. The nun saw me struggling and approached my desk. I explained the problem. She took my hand, put the two handles in its grasp and said, "If I wanted to carry it for Sister, I'd carry it this way. If I didn't want to carry it for Sister, I wouldn't know how to carry it."

Why no meow?

My father believed that emptying a can of Mystery Oil into his carburetor would improve gas mileage. Although I was ten, my father made me sit behind the wheel, turn on the ignition and step on the gas pedal while he poured. Black smoke coughed out of the exhaust pipe and literally covered the street. No car could pass; no pedestrian could see. It was an embarrassment to my mother and they fought over it. To keep from having another fight a few months later, my father took me to another part of the neighborhood. He chose the P.S. 89 schoolyard at lunch hour, when the basketball courts and playground swarmed with children. As I pumped the pedal, smoke smothered the kids, making them invisible, their presence known only by the coughing and screaming, the cries we heard as we drove away.

The guest host of the television show, *Greater Boston*, moderated a discussion on the subject of anti-abortion political candidates showing graphic photos of aborted babies. Asked for his own opinion, he said he was "deeply ambivalent."

Dear Mr. Skoyles:

Please allow me to take your poetry workshop. I do not want to have Professor Bill Knott throw another thesaurus at my head.

Yours,
Arthur Leed

Artist David Cerny was commissioned by the Czech Republic to commemorate its presidency of the Council of the European Union. Cerny's 172-square-foot, eight-ton sculpture, *Entropa*, is comprised of a kind of jig-saw puzzle of twenty-seven pieces, each, he said, done by a different artist from each of the twenty-seven states of the European Union.

Unveiled in Prague in 2009, the piece shocked government officials with its images of the countries, not by the assorted artists, but all by Cerny in an enormous hoax. These were among those represented:

> Belgium: A half-full box of half-eaten chocolates.
> Bulgaria: A string of toilets lighted by neon.
> Germany: A series of highways resembling a
>   swastika.
> Italy: Soccer players holding balls against
>   which they appear to be masturbating.
> Luxembourg: A gold nugget mounted with a
>   For Sale sign.
> The Netherlands has disappeared under the sea.

My neighbor's huge mobile home was spacious and luxurious. He told me the gas mileage was 9 miles per gallon. "Not much for a car, but a lot for a house," he said, probably repeating the salesman's line.

Moondog, a heavily bearded man dressed in wrapped sandals, a horned helmet and Viking robes, stood for years centurion-like on the corner of 54th Street and 6th Avenue. He held a long spear and sold poetry and essays about musical philosophy. I met him when I was sixteen, working as a messenger for Paramount Pictures. I had saved fifteen cents by walking instead of using the carfare provided by the head of the mailroom. I gave Moondog the money and he told me to choose from the packets of pages hanging from his sword. When I put the coins in his hand I noticed he was blind. Across the street was a wooden newsstand whose owner was also blind, and he began waving at us. I mentioned this to Moondog and he thanked me, left for the west side of 6th Avenue where he sat down for lunch with his friend. I read the essay about his music, composed in "snaketime," in what he called a "slithery rhythm."

During a residency at Yaddo, I met Tobias Schneebaum, author of *Keep the River on Your Right*. He had lived with the Harakmbut tribe of headhunters, and said he had eaten human flesh. I wanted to ask him how it tasted, but never had the chance. A year later, in Paris, I saw him leaning on a post outside the Follies Bergère. He said he had just come from Singapore where a three-course meal costs fifty cents. I posed my question.

"Like pork," he said.

One of my colleagues fell from a horse, hit his head and was not the same. He could be seen leaving his office on the way to the lecture hall with a long extension cord hanging from the back of his pants, where it had been attached to a heating pad. He became more and more forgetful, and finally was called into the dean's office after giving failing grades to everyone in his classes. When the dean questioned him, he said that the students were not authentic. Pressed, he said they did not really exist. The dean called two student workers into his office and asked what was unreal about them.

"Hastily put up men," he replied sadly, looking them over. "Hastily put up men."

I was sent by God to torment myself, my relatives and those tormented by sin.

When I am dead, when I can finally concentrate.

My friend the gravedigger told me that a sculptor named Cutler, whose work consisted entirely of hair, had bought a plot in the Provincetown graveyard. But a few weeks later, Cutler discovered the plot alongside Robert Motherwell was available, and he switched his gravesite to be near the celebrated artist. Proving there is social climbing even in the afterlife.

The elephant skin lady in the sideshow said about the sword swallower, "To the public he's a freak, but to the freaks he's not a freak."

Norman Mailer's blurb for the novel *Crust*: "It's wild as sin and revolting as vomit and as exceptional as the lower reaches of hell itself."

I don't blab no drab gab. I chatter hep patter.

We were cruel children and Mr. Bluett was one of our favorite targets. He was a little crazy, and in winter wore plastic bags over his shoes and socks for gloves. When he came out of his house, we chanted:

>Socks on the hands!
>Bags on the feet!

Our favorite pastime was to go through the garbage cans that lined the street twice a week. One morning we found a trove of art supplies: tubes of paint, bottles of ink. We smeared paint and pitched the bottles as hard as we could against Mr. Bluett's house, making the siding an explosion of color and broken glass. An older kid found a brush and drew an outline of an enormous breast—we were amazed—it was perfect and realistic and we stood before it breathless.

Our furious, embarrassed mothers ordered us to scrub up the mess, and stood by while we sloshed buckets of ammonia and wiped and rubbed the siding clean. One mother went further and demanded to know the painter of the breast, saying, "Who drew that disgusting thing?" The culprit admitted it, but claimed innocence by saying, to our surprise, "It's a lung!" He kept repeating it over and over until we were all yelling the same thing in his defense, in chorus, "It's a lung! It's just a lung!"

Roy Radin became a millionaire before he was twenty by assembling a touring vaudeville troupe which consisted of J. Fred Muggs, the chimpanzee from the *Today* show; a midget saxophone player; a drag queen magician; and George Jessel.

There was a huge snowstorm and no one could get on the road. We lost power and phone lines. Everyone was stranded for five days. When it was over, I called Judy Shahn, saying how awful it was. But she had had a good time. She had finished some prints and Dugan wrote some new poems.

I had been reading a philosopher who said that an artist, because he's so involved in his work, is a person who doesn't truly live. This proved the opposite—the artist is a person who lives doubly—twice as much. He has an interior life as well as the one visible to the world.

The poet Attila József lived in poverty. He wrote a letter to a foundation requesting a grant. He said he would use the funds to buy cigarettes. He said that those reading his proposal would probably be wondering why he wasn't asking for money for food. He said it was because he had already gotten used to being hungry.

Dear Mr. Big-Shot Artist:

The punk band, Orchid, referred your email to my office, as I represent, pro bono, many groups on independent labels, who cannot afford counsel. I do this in my spare time, which is why I write on a Sunday night.

I understand that you are concerned that your Ovid illustration was used by the band without your permission, thereby infringing on your copyright. While I recognize your generosity in requesting only a "demo" in return, I must tell you there is no demo, only the final product. A "demo" is made only by premier rock 'n'rollers who send it on to labels owned by men who also own airlines and software companies, and then the demo, if purchased, is professionally produced. In the case of Orchid, there is only one version, the original and final product. To suggest that Orchid makes "demos" is to grossly overestimate their wealth and standing.

Further, you referred to the release as *Pig Destroyer*. For your information, the record has Orchid on one side, and a band called Pig Destroyer on the flip. The release by Orchid is self-titled.

If you have a beef with Pig Destroyer, please take it up with them.

Your email says, "I hear you guys are wild." If you knew anything about Orchid, you would know they are far from "wild," whatever that means to you. These are polite, educated and community-oriented musicians. At 9/11, they moved to New York to play benefits for victims of the disaster.

What exactly do you want? I feel you are angling for more than the "demo." Please be specific when you reply, but let me be up front: I don't think you're going to get much from a band who has never made a dime from its work.

And frankly, I'm not an art critic, but the image you are creating a stir about looks to me like a barbecue fork stuck into a hot dog with arms and legs. How much do you expect for that, Mr. Big Shot?

When you reply, please get real.

Mark Colletti
Colletti, Colletti and Epstein

Attila József threw himself onto the railroad tracks and was killed by an oncoming train when he was thirty-two.

The museum where women are portrayed cubically.

My tenure-seeking colleague came to my office with a story he tossed on my desk.

"Tell me what you think," he asked.

I read the first sentence, *Outside, a sailor bargained for the charms of a shopworn streetwalker.*

My name is Mary, but everyone calls me Captain Cook's widow.

Jones told of being the only American to witness a beheading in the village of a New Guinea tribe. He said when the eyes of the decapitated head followed him as it rolled, they made him a prince.

One night at McSorley's, Burkie was praising his literature teacher to his poet friends, saying, "Chekhov would be just another writer if she hadn't made him personal by her love of him. Ditto Gogol." Blanche wanted "Ditto Gogol" as a title for one of her poems, and Burkie said she could have it, but only in exchange for the words on the receipt she had showed him from her purchase of

22

Bachelard's *The Psychoanalysis of Fire* and *The Poetics of Reverie* at the Strand Bookstore: *2 Bachelard.*

In fifth grade, I was the best player in the St. Bartholomew's Chess Club. One Saturday morning, Brother Dominic, the club founder, arranged for Montecarlo Rosetti, a grandmaster, to give a talk and then play the entire class at once. Twenty of us set up in the cafeteria and Rosetti went from game to game, leaning over each board, making a move and shuffling onto the next. After an hour, I called Brother Dominic. I had the grandmaster in checkmate. Dominic looked me in the eye and said it was impossible, but when he studied my board, he ran off to get another teacher. Mr. Dwyer came to the same conclusion. Soon word spread to the parents and siblings of the players who watched from the circumference. I composed myself as best I could when Mr. Rosetti leaned over my board. I moved my bishop, and, in as polite a tone as I could muster, quelling my excitement, I said, "*Check*, and, I believe, *Mate.*"

Rosetti was shocked. He stood up straight and linked his hands behind his back. He looked left and right, then leaned over the board once more and stared at me.

"That is a very shrewd move," he said. "And you would be well advised to make it. However, it is *my* turn."

Babette was completely demented and given to saying the craziest things which made no sense. I tried with all my might to understand the content of her abstruse utterances. She would say, "I am the Lorelai." Or would wail, "I am Socrates' deputy." Yet absurd outbursts like, "I am the double polytechnic irreplaceable" or "I am plum cake on a corn meal bottom" or "I am Germania and Helvetia of exclusively sweet butter" or "Naples and I must supply the world with noodles," signify an increase in her self-valuation, that is to say, a compensation for inferiority feelings.

Emily Hahn's *Romantic Rebels: An Informal History of Bohemianism in America*, cost an extravagant $5.95 when I was a kid, but I saved up for it because in her author's photo she held a cigar.

The dean approved a sabbatical proposal to track the outcomes of previous sabbaticals.

The front of the martial arts expert's t-shirt said *The Pistol Club*, so I guessed he had moved from nunchuks to firearms, but when he turned, the lettering on the back read *Drink All Night, Pistol Dawn.*

At a New York City festival honoring Borges, celebrated poets from across the country read their favorite Borges poem, and he commented after each. One poet finished reading his choice with great feeling, and Borges thanked him, saying he liked that poem very much, but that it was a poem by Ralph Waldo Emerson that he had translated into Spanish.

> Oh to be seventeen years old
> Once again… and not know that poetry

is ruled with the scepter of the dumb, the deaf and
    the creepy!

I decided to kill myself. I had my gun license and a legal
hand gun, a revolver. I sat at my desk and shuffled my
books, including those by Joyce, an echo of a similar
experience from another age. I opened the *Portrait* to
Stephen leaving his house, walking down a lane and
hearing "a mad nun screeching in the nuns' madhouse
beyond the wall,

    —Jesus! O Jesus! Jesus!"

and I wanted to yell that desperate prayer, or was it a
curse, a cry? A plea to the empty sky? The full heavens?
Whatever it was, I wanted to howl it myself, out the window and into the avenue, in the voice of that crazy sister, the one person who made me feel less alone, and I
decided to live.

My friend and his twin had grown apart since their mar-
riages, moved to different cities, and saw each other only
on an occasional holiday. Business took them separately
to London, and my friend went to an antiquarian bookstore, having become interested in the history of cavalry
formations. He walked the aisles, located the right section, his index finger travelling the spines, until he found
the book he sought by Robert Hewes. As he was about
to lift *An Elucidation of Regulations for the Formations and
Movements of Cavalry* from the shelf, he was interrupted
by another hand reaching for the same volume, a person
he hadn't noticed, his twin.

I went back to my neighborhood in Queens, to the block I grew up on, Judge Street. Much had changed in twenty-five years. All the front yards had been paved for parking spaces. Steel bars guarded the windows of first-floor apartments. I saw a woman I recognized from my childhood. I never knew her name, just used to see her walking an Airedale morning and night. She had lived in a apartment house on nearby Elmhurst Avenue. She was an old lady now, with a poodle. I reached the end of my former street and, as I was about to cross, she waved. I was puzzled—she couldn't have recognized me. She rushed up, excited, looked at me, a little dazed, and said, "Can you tell me how to get to Elmhurst Avenue?" And I told her.

I arrived in Paris and found a hotel for the night. As soon as I entered my room, the phone rang. A woman with a French accent said, "John?" I said yes, amazed that anyone knew I was here, as I didn't know myself until a moment ago. She said she just wanted to say how much she liked me, that she hoped we could see each other. She went on and on, nervously, breathlessly, mentioning the Jardin des Tuileries, until I finally got a word in and asked who she was. She said, "Aren't you the John I met earlier this afternoon?" She had fallen in love with an American named John and was calling every hotel in Paris, asking for every John who was registered there, hoping to find him.

John,

One Saturday early in the eighth grade I went crazy. I had hair growing out of one armpit and not the other. That morning there was band practice and a girl scout meeting in the old school gym. Outside was track practice. I was with some friend and we dared each other to be cool. I plucked a feather out of an ornate band helmet and waited for them to play a set. Then I went from one member to another in the back row and tortured them with the feather. When that wasn't fun anymore, I went outside where the track team was practicing how to use starting blocks. When the gun went off, I was behind them. I reached and held heels. After awhile this bored me too, so we found a rope and stretched it ankle-high across the top of the stairs leading down to the gym.

I've never been real smart, so I was truly surprised the following Monday. Right off, I found out I was kicked off the track team, and that there would be an emergency meeting of the altar boys after school. On the way to that meeting I saw John Truber's little brother Brian. My little sister Eleanor would tell me if Brian so much as gave her a dirty look. He was one dog I could catch and often did.

When I walked in the church Father Green pointed at me and said "Don't even sit down, just get out of here!"

I went home and studied the matter. Soon I heard something and looked outside. Brian Truber was on the street screaming, "MATTLIN GOT KICKED OFF THE ALTAR BOYS."

Funny thing, I never saw that rat again even though he lived across the street.

My mother heard and that night Mom took her *South Pacific* record out of the Victrola and Pop cut a half-inch stick from the backyard hedges. I was stretched over the cabinet and whipped on the back of the legs.

Some months later the letters came in from all the Catholic schools I applied to and every one said no. Mom knew right off that Newtown High was nothing more than a step toward Sing Sing, so she dragged me to the Friary and begged for clemency.

They put me in a school the brothers ran for retarded and disturbed boys, St. Leonard's Academy. I moved on to a diploma from St. John's Prep, a degree from St. Francis College, and now work as an artillery surveyor aiming nuclear missiles at the Soviets. I have regained my balance. God be with you.

Best,
Jackie Mattlin

The worst thing that happens in some people's lives might also be the only thing.

Dear Professor:

Thank you yet again for helping me get accepted into Utrecht University in the Netherlands.

After one term, I regret that I have decided to unroll from this place as I did from JeJu National. It was worth it to learn that philosophy is an individual sport and should be studied alone. I met many brave questioners and professors, but they all seemed to be pushing me toward my own way.

And so I am on that way now! And with your help!

Thank you again for your patience and the trial of your support.

Your former student,
Bertrand

Pessimism of the intellect. Optimism of the will.

The French translation of the title of James Crumley's book, *Murder in the Topless Bar* translates back into English as *Murder in the House without a Roof.*

The retired Victorian professor did not answer his phone, so I called the department chair, and we went to his house. When we arrived at the street number, it was an apartment building, not the mansion he had described so beautifully and in such detail all year. We were certain we had the wrong place, but his name was on the plate in the lobby.

The superintendent let us into a drab studio, with wall to wall bookcases stacked with decades of student papers and theses. Our colleague lay on the floor in front of a television screen of static. I cupped the back of his head with my hand and the chairman took his pulse as the super called for an ambulance. Medics arrived and took him away.

The chairman and I left, discussing the fantastic fictional stories he had invented over the past year. We visited him the next day in the hospital. Before he lapsed into a coma, he said, "They don't even know who Ozymandias is."

The life we didn't choose to lead, that's our real life.

I consider it obscene and barbaric that our poetic institutions like the Academy of American Poets, the Poetry Society of America, the Poetry Foundation *et al.*, that they have no euthanasic programs to help elderly poets in our hour of need. I have no reason to continue past next May, no family, no wife, no children. Nothing but poems which means no poems because every failed poet quits in the end, and if they don't quit, if we don't quit, then we're fools, which I refuse to be, I refuse to live as a failed poet, a fool...

I had a plan a couple years ago, when my Social Security payments began, and I noticed in their official forms that my spouse, my never-was spouse, would receive survivor benefits when I died, with the proviso that they (she) were required to have been married for at least one year to the decedent. So I asked everybody I knew if they knew of an older woman poet of impoverished means, who might marry me (in name only of course, a *marriage blanc*, no cohabitation or contact necessary) in order to collect the benefits when I died a year and a day after the wedding, but there were none to be found. Like all the hopes and schemes of my life this too went unrealized.

So my Social Security payments will go to waste. My lifetime of small paychecks adding up over the decades to something nothing, a pittance, two thousand dollars a month for the rest of my life which is no life and which must at some as yet undetermined time after May 2008 be cancelled because without the poetry I can't live.

Poetry is the wealth that poverty brings.

We moved near Wellfleet, the town where Marconi transmitted his first radio message, and I got my ham license (KB1JUJ. Kilo Bravo One Juliet Uniform Juliet), a modest radio and an antenna, the equipment I needed to talk with people all over the world. But when I reached them, they only wanted to discuss their equipment.

I saw Chapman at an Arabian Horse Show in Fort Worth (he married the richest woman in Louisiana, who is also the ugliest women in Louisiana). He told me then, at the horse show, that he had "detached from reality for a while" but that he was OK now. But the truth is he seemed crazy as hell to me. He runs a Koi farm…

Could a greater miracle take place than for us to look through each other's eyes for an instant?

> Doctor, doctor, give me the news
> I got a bad case of lovin' you

My son's sixth grade teacher posts a sign in the classroom: BETTER A DIAMOND WITH A FLAW THAN A PEBBLE WITHOUT. The author is given as *Ibid*.

I taught in Dallas, at Southern Methodist University, and in my class was an African-American student, my age, twenty-six. We occasionally went out to dinner together in restaurants near the college. Several times, free drinks arrived at our table, sent over by another patron, and the student would look across the room and raise his glass to the benefactor. I thought he must have had many friends in the city, but when this happened for the third time, I asked him about it and he said that customers were not used to seeing a black man in that part of town, and each one who bought the drinks assumed he was a member of the Dallas Cowboys.

These are the schnitzels.

The dean came to an English department meeting and suggested sexier names for courses. She said, "Literary Foundations: Sophocles, Plato and Others," was dull. A colleague suggested, "Last Tango in Athens."

Respectability is one hell of a great disguise.

Poet Karl Shapiro opposed Pound receiving the Bollingen Prize on the grounds of his anti-Semitism. Many in the literary community criticized Shapiro for this stand. He called his next book, *Poems of a Jew.*

Criticized for writing about bourgeois subjects, he called his next book, *The Bourgeois Poet.*

When the *New York Times* crossword puzzle hinted at Shapiro's identity with the clue, "late U.S. poet," and the American Medical Association listed him as a suicide, he called his autobiography, *Reports of My Death.*

David Markson collected anti-Semites.

My friend's teenage son, diagnosed with Obsessive Compulsive Disorder, feared going bald. He spent hours at the mirror, lifting the bangs from his forehead, checking to see if his hairline was receding. My friend sent him to a dermatologist who told him he wasn't going bald, that it was natural at all ages for hair to fall out and regenerate. To prove this to him, she suggested he count the hairs on his pillow each morning, with the result that the boy did not go bald, he went mad.

A Gestapo officer came to Picasso's studio, saw a photograph of his *Guernica* on the wall, and asked him, "Did you do that?"

Picasso said, "No, you did."

John Lennon said he heard Elvis sing, *Uh-huh, Um-Um, Yeah-Yeah*, in a refrain. He said he had heard, *Uh-huh* before as well as *Um-Um* and *Yeah-Yeah*, but never all three together. Then Lennon wrote, "She Loves You," with its three yeahs.

When my small son gets excited, he adds an extra stressed syllable to that poetic foot, the spondee, changing it from, "Da-da!" to "Da-da-da!"

Allan Miller directed a short film of the painter Paul Resika working on a canvas. The artist first draws in charcoal. Then he paints the outline of a boat, puts in the sea and a moon. This goes on for days. For the rest of the film he keeps changing the form and the colors. The moon is placed in several differently colored skies. At the end, there is no moon. At one point, he finds the color he was looking for—a bright yellow. He says, "That's it!"—the first glimmer of happiness in the film. He puts it in, and then he sits back and lights a small cigar. He now sees that a milder yellow he had used before is now overwhelmed by the new yellow. He smiles and says, "That yellow has stolen the other yellow's stuff. Well, what can you do? Another girl walked into the room…"

Rodin was solitary before he became famous, and after he became famous, he was even more solitary, because what is fame but the accumulation of misunderstandings that surround a name?

At the beginning of each class, the art school professor wrote on the board: Clarity and Surprise.

Turgenev was a student in Nikolai Gogol's history class, an appointment Gogol obtained through friends though he was completely ignorant of the subject. Gogol missed most classes and those he attended consisted of his unfurling maps and speaking vaguely about the countries whose outlines on the wall he tapped with a pointer. He showed up for the required final oral exam with his head wrapped in a bandage and complaining of a toothache. Another professor had to ask the questions.

Of this time, Gogol said, "Unrecognized I mounted the rostrum, and unrecognized I descended from it."

Turgenev wrote that Gogol was to be the teacher of his generation, but it would not take place in a university classroom.

Oh, for Christ's sake, one doesn't *study* poets! You read them, and think, *That's great, how is it done? Could I do it?* and that's how you learn.

Your name and mine inside a heart upon a wall
Still finds a way to haunt me though they're so small.

On hearing that I graduated from college, my neighbor, an Italian housepainter, said, "Congratulations, Johnny. Keep a push, a push, a push, and someday, you'll reach-a the point."

My Italian grandmother used to sing, "Where Do You Work-A, John?"

Long time ago, John and-a Joe
Come from sunny Italy
To-a try-a to get-a the dough.
Joe go away, John he's-a stay,
When they meet the other day,
Here's-a what-a they got-a to say:

Where do you work-a, John?
On the Delaware Lackawan.
What do you do-a, John?
I push-a, push-a, push.
What do you push-a, John?
I push, I push-a da truck,
Where do you push-a, John?
On the Delaware Lackawan-awan-awan-awan,
The Delaware Lackawan.

Written by Harry Warren, whose real name was Salvatore Antonio Guaragna.

Charlie Frazier and I were drinking in a bar in Queens called The Apollo 12 Moon Landing when a song called "You'll Never Walk Alone" played on the jukebox. My friend said his father loved that song, and when he was born, his father gave him that song as his theme song. My friend sang along with it, "Walk on through the wind, / walk on through the rain, / though your dreams be tossed and blown. / Walk on, walk on / with hope in your heart / and you'll never walk alone." He looked into his beer glass and said, "And that's just what I've gone and done."

"No one drives the Frazier-mobile, but Frazier," said Frazier.

In grammar school, Sister Grace Winifred gave each student in our first grade class a square of paper to which she had taped little piece of lint, a relic, that "had been touched to a bone of Blessed Martin."

Lou Berrone, my favorite college professor, specialized in Irish literature. He lived for Joyce and we lived for his stories about his friends in Westport which included composers, artists and writers. He described the Pequot Library, the Remarkable Bookshop and Viva Zapata's restaurant where at closing time the eccentric owner turned a hose on lingering diners.

He told tall tales, or tales that seemed tall to an undergraduate. When a student quoted the critic Zack Bowen, Berrone thrust his palm forward like a cop halting traffic and told of a ten-course feast he had enjoyed with that scholar. At the mention of Nathan Halper, Berrone recalled buying a painting from him at Halper's HCE Gallery, which was named after a character in *Finnegan's Wake*. When the Joyce Society hosted a lecture upstairs from the Gotham Book Mart, I attended, and Berrone introduced me to both men. Until then, I didn't believe these people existed. They were simply bibliographical entries quoted to support or refute academic points.

Still, his namedropping and boasts about the strange people he knew (his best friend's grandfather invented the pinwheel) left me and some classmates wondering.

In my senior year, he announced, "I am the only man in the world who knows that Joyce wrote two essays which are in the archives of the University of Padua!" He noted that even Richard Ellmann, author of the definitive biography of Joyce, was unaware of this find.

We left class shaking our heads. Padua? Something Ellmann missed?

After graduation, I opened the *New York Times* to the headline, "Unpublished Work by Joyce Is Found," and the article told of Berrone's discovery. The piece ended with Ellmann saying he "envied the man who found them." Random House published his book on the subject.

Decades later, I was discussing Joyce with a colleague and decided to contact Berrone. I tracked him to a Senior Center in Pennsylvania. His voice on the phone was still full of curiosity and wit. I reminded him of our seminar in *Ulysses* and he remembered there were eighteen students, the number of chapters in the novel. He expressed his continued love of Joyce, and his paper comparing Joyce's prose to the façade of a gothic cathedral. He easily could have been back at the rostrum, and I wanted to tell everyone about my old teacher, newly found, who was still teaching. I suggested having my Boston colleague, the one who taught the history of the novel, give him a call and Berrone was open to the possibility.

He suddenly became personal, telling me things about his childhood. He had been blind from ages eight to ten, and read every Braille book in his small home town library. During that time he studied singing and at eleven he developed a tenor voice and sang at the Oak Room of the Plaza Hotel where Betty Davis heard him and invited him to her mansion. He had been interviewed ten times by John Cameron Swayze on NBC TV; George Bernard Shaw, impressed, sent a limousine which drove him to Shaw's place in Maine where Berrone beat him at tennis. Gandhi befriended him and he visited India often, playing field hockey with Indira.

I was speechless. I asked if he had written anything about his childhood, or if his children had recorded his life? He said that wasn't important, that since he was approaching ninety, the next day was all that mattered.

I couldn't wait to tell my wife. At dinner that night, I burst out with it, that I had contacted my old teacher, we had talked for over an hour, and I learned about his extraordinary youth—a boy tenor, beating GBS at tennis, flown to India by Gandhi...

"Are you kidding?" she asked.

I was ready to defend him, to make up for my past doubt, but as she looked at me, puzzled, I started to recall other details. His blinding was by an Italian waiter who threw red vinegar at him because his father was a spokesman for FDR and the waiter a Fascist general. He had directed Elizabeth "*Violet Eyes*" Taylor in Westport, and Meryl Streep when she was a student at the Yale

Drama School. He won the Hartford Open Golf Tournament three times.

Still, I told my wife the unlikely story of the Paduan essays, and that maybe… no, I had to admit….

Four things an older man must never say to a younger woman:

1. What did you say?
2. What's your name again?
3. Is it cold in here?
4. Is it hot in here?

His credentials in the field of creative writing amount to three short-short stories published in small magazines between 2002 and 2007, a found poem from a Denny's menu and a haiku in an online journal. The article on fish imagery in *Lawrence of Arabia* displays sound scholarship, but this single entity falls far short of the six articles required for tenure. The promising manuscript, *Lives of the Poets for Children*, is far from complete, containing just four entries. He has written but not published pornographic stories whose main subject is incest, and has started a novel which begins with the sentence: *Carlos woke with a jerk.*

The committee regretfully concludes it cannot support his application for tenure.

George Herbert Walker Bush gave the graduation speech at Warren Wilson College when he was vice president. Before the ceremony, several of us in the platform party sat with him and the discussion turned to an electrical fire that recently destroyed a colleague's home on campus. Bush said he knew how the man must feel because after graduating from Yale and starting his own fossil fuel company in Texas, one of his oil rigs caught fire and sank in the Gulf of Mexico.

PEN SELLER: Here is something once offered on this site but surprisingly no takers as this item is out of this world, and I mean this literally. Here is the legendary truly limited edition Parker ballpoint space pen that one rarely sees in a lifetime. The pen comes with the rare limited pressed 45 record to be played when you sip your drink of choice and hold and behold a pen that once went to the moon. Step up on this likely once in a lifetime chance to own this special item that is guaranteed to have heads turning in the pen circuit. The price, excluding shipping is $2,500.

INTERESTED PARTY: Please show where your documentation shows that this pen "went to the moon"?

PEN SELLER: The entire pen of course did not go to the moon. The material used for the top part of this ballpoint, the clicker as it were, was taken from the rocket that launched John Glenn. I refer you to the two articles cited for further reading, thank you for your interest.

ANOTHER INTERESTED PARTY: "The entire pen of course did not go to the moon." This is very different than what you wrote in your for sale announcement, where you described it as the pen that went to the moon. In fact, reading your second sentence it turns out that none of it went to the moon. A very small part of the pen, the clicker, came from a rocket that launched John Glenn.

The launching rocket, of course, drops away. And John Glenn himself never went to the moon. He was the first American to orbit the Earth, but he never went to the moon. I admire your expertise, and especially your attempt to create an animal shelter, but misleading descriptions are not helpful.

A Pentel mechanical pencil lies on my desk. I got it in Cambridge. I was outside the Harvard Coop, leaning against a tree and reading my list of things to buy before leaving town. On that list: mechanical pencil. I was about to enter the store when I found this pencil by the edge of my sneaker.

Carlos Fuentes said that in Latin America even the atheists are Catholics.

It was as if an occult hand had reached down from above and moved the players like pawns upon some giant chessboard.

I had to report to the Selective Service station in New Haven. A hundred of us sat at little desks to fill out a short form. One section asked us to check boxes signifying membership in various organizations. I was a member of the Students for a Democratic Society, but it wasn't on the list. Nor were the Black Panthers. Among those to choose from were The Knights of the White Camelia and The Sons of Liberty. Many complained about the Panthers not being present, as the Panthers had a large following in New Haven. The sergeant said, "Just what's on the list." Then he instructed us to leave blank Question 11, which asked, "Have you had homosexual experience?" We handed in our forms. At the end of the day, after we were given physicals, our papers were returned to us just so we could sign them and hand them in once more. Question 11 had been checked negatively for everyone in the room, and everyone was drafted.

> Go over and over your beads, paint designs on
>   your forehead,
> wear your hair matted, long and ostentatious,
> but when deep inside you there's a loaded gun,
>   how can you have God?

The censored version of a script included the change from "That's what happens when you fuck a stranger in the ass," to "That's what happens when you meet a stranger in the alps."

In grade school, I was friends with the son of Mr. Feld, who ran a funeral home, and whose wife had died. I hated to be invited for dinner because the house was always frigid, in all seasons. And the food was cold too—cold soup and cold cuts. Ice cream. One very cold day in January, he saw me walking down the street in the snow and gave me a ride in his Cadillac which had the air conditioning so high I could see my breath.

A gust of wind fatally knocked Papa Wallenda of the Flying Wallendas from a high wire strung over an avenue in Puerto Rico. The next day's headline read, "Papa Wallenda Blown to Death."

It's hard to define *good*. A son who shoots his mother from a hundred yards away might be a good shot, but not a good son.

I grew up in Queens at the time of the razing of single family homes and the building of apartment houses. This meant great fun for us kids, as we entered vacant houses, taking objects left behind like stray silverware, shirts, sheets we tied in knots. And breaking windows and mirrors. Our mothers warned us about the dangers of the foul puddles in cellars which could give us polio, or shaky staircases from which we could fall. They did not prepare us for the fact that three boys were found dead in an upstairs bedroom, each sitting on the floor, their backs against the wall, their temples punctured with an ice pick and, over each of their heads, their names printed in blood.

The martini is womankind's most devoted ally. Martinis make all women beautiful to the beholder who succumbs to the most diabolical of all cocktails. The martini will do more for a homely broad's ego than plastic surgery or psychiatry. The martini lush is incapable of any act more strenuous than the raising of his glass. In some cases the olive is omitted because the added weight would make it impossible for the consumer to lift the potion. If seated, the martini drunk has as much chance of rising as a raincoat flung over the back of a chair. The martini flirtation is seldom soiled by an embrace.

Eddie Condon said that Bix Beiderbecke's cornet solos sounded like a girl saying yes.

All fleas dream of buying a dog.

But what about your teaching, Charlie?

My friend's son enjoyed diving onto their cat when curled up on the couch, so that it awoke with a yowl. My friend explained to his son that he might not realize it, but this hurt kitty, and so he shouldn't do it anymore. The boy said, "But I *want* to hurt kitty."

Why no meow?

INRI   Iron Nails Rammed In

The dean asked us to stress critical thinking in each of our courses. It was no different from my Italian grandfather, a uneducated man who worked as a roofer, saying to his children, when they did something stupid, "Hey, use-a your head!"

The 1968 presidential race saw three candidates: Richard Nixon, Hubert Humphrey and George Wallace. Julian Bond, the first African-American to be proposed for the vice presidency, said the difference among the three candidates was:

    Wallace would drive over him.
    Nixon would watch Wallace drive over him.
    Humphrey would cry as Wallace drove over him.

The patient taking the Rorschach test giggled uncontrollably at the first several inkblots, but after a dozen, he became hysterical, asking, "Where in the world did you get such filthy pictures?"

John Cheever came to the Fine Arts Work Center, and had his photograph taken with the Writing Fellows. As ten of us stood around him, and the photographer aimed his camera, Cheever said, "Say Cheever!"

To claim that a book is a novel, an allegory, or a treatise on aesthetics has more or less the same value as saying that it has a yellow cover and can be found on the third shelf to the left.

At a cocktail party of aesthetes, the host said that man's worst invention was the ball.
    "Next, the guitar," another said.
    "And then the guitar solo," the host added.

"You haven't had a hangover, until you've had a hangover at reveille," the soldier said.

A well-known novelist in his fifties dated the young and beautiful hostess he met at a local restaurant. The three of us were driving together in his Porsche when he said, "My turn signal stopped working," and he fiddled with it. "Oh, good," he said, "I can still use it manually."
    The girl said, "For God's sake, why can't you just say *by hand*."

My uncle called me and said he had something very important to tell me.
    "Are you sitting down?" he asked.

I knew his wife had been ill and feared the worst.

"Just tell me," I said.

"Are you sitting down?" he repeated. "We're Jewish! My daughter had the Bertolotti genome traced and we're Italian Jews! Are you there? Are you all right?"

The dean returned from her vacation and talked about the peace and quiet she enjoyed in Vermont. She said it was so different from Boston's honking horns and police sirens—just a silence interrupted only by bird-song. Walking in the woods, she said she heard a hermit thrush. She was never more eloquent, describing the song as hesitant and crystalline, saying she looked it up and found a poem on the bird by Amy Clampitt. I wondered if the time away had really recharged her, but then she continued, calling it a thermit hush and a kermit thrush, as if the conference room had once again taken over and confusion reigned.

Jonathan wanted to be someone else, so he changed his name to Janaka. Alice felt the same and became Alish. So John became Gian. Marianne became Marika, and Deborah, Debka, but you can't get drunk by reading the labels on bottles.

The Daily Express, on the death of Brendan Behan at 41: TOO YOUNG TO DIE BUT TOO DRUNK TO LIVE.

I had dinner with a friend at Bill Zuber's Yankee restaurant in Iowa's Amana colony, an area known for its pork. It was a beautiful spring evening, and a woman and her two little girls, in pink and yellow dresses, approached the fence near the parking lot where large sows grunted. The largest of them turned and kicked mud onto the three of them. The girls were too shocked to cry, their dresses spoiled. The mother comforted them, saying it was only natural, adding, "That's why they call them piggies."

My son and I sat on the grass at a Cape Cod League base-ball game in Orleans. We got there early, and he was reading aloud the signs on the trucks.

"Sandwich," he said. "I wonder where that word comes from."

The teenage boy behind us said to his friend, "Did you hear that kid? He asked where a word comes from? Where do any words come from?"

The baby is made of milk. The grape is made of wine.

Every Tuesday I took the bus from Cape Cod to Boston, a two-hour trip. I waited with Lee, a web designer for Citizens Bank. One morning he said that almost all of the independent contractors were let go the night before by email. He was told he'd know his fate by 8:30. The bus left at 8:10, so he felt he had to go in, in case he was one of the survivors. He always sat in the front and I sat in the back. I could see him fidgeting with his phone, checking it every few minutes. When we got off, he told me he, too, had been fired. He said it was hard to be fired on the bus.

Only later did I learn how many internal fractures were concealed by his apparent normality.

Survived by his wife.

Frank O'Hara and Larry Rivers descended the stairs at the City Center, during the intermission of a performance of a ballet, and an art dealer yelled, "Here they are, all covered in blood and semen." A remark said about Rimbaud and Verlaine a hundred years earlier.

To hold a pen is to be at war.

The electrician at the art center I directed kissed one of the female residents when leaving her apartment after repairing a faulty outlet. She complained to me but said she didn't want him fired, just warned. I did so and he apologized to her, but a week later he showed up at her door at midnight with a bottle of wine. She had a hard time getting him out. On Monday, I told him I had to let him go, as none of the other women in residence wanted him near their apartments. When the president of the board of trustees, a female artist in her eighties, found out, she was upset with my decision, and said, "Don't women have elbows anymore?"

After claiming he was stopped by both local and state police due to his bumper sticker I SPIT ON THE SUPREME COURT, our local libertarian covered it up with HONK IF YOU LOVE HONKING.

Albert DeSalvo, who confessed to being the serial killer known as the Boston Strangler, made costume jewelry while serving time in Walpole State Prison, specializing in choker necklaces.

Joseph Brodsky told me his two favorite pop songs were "Jeepers, Creepers" and "Walk Away Renee."

Ray Carver team-taught fiction workshops with Geoffrey Wolff at Goddard's low-residency MFA Program. Geoffrey said Ray often arrived in class with a hangover. Because he hadn't read the stories, he always began by talking about the title, noting that the title was the most important part of the story, in the same way that the roof is the most important part of your house because it is the first thing a visitor sees when he arrives. Geoffrey said he listened to this for years before realizing that the roof is not the first thing a visitor sees.

A house has a beginning, a middle and an end, but not necessarily in that order.

It's more important to love your house than to love your country.

I babysat for a couple's toddler while they went to dinner. An hour after they left, the little boy tripped, and started crying. I picked him up to console him while he continued yelling through his tears something I couldn't understand. I brought him a glass of water, juggled a stuffed penguin in front of his face and walked him around. He was still crying and talking incomprehensibly when his parents returned. His mother told me he was saying, "Dry my tears."

Hope makes a good breakfast but a poor dinner.

From first grade through eighth, students at St. Bartholomew's Grammar School attended mass on the first Friday morning of each month. Doctrine said that if we received communion nine months in a row, we would die in the company of a priest, assuring us of heaven. Our third grade teacher, Sister Mary Helene, said that if we accomplished this, our "tepid souls would grow fervent."

After mass one Friday, I realized that I'd left my lunch box in the pew. I walked back and saw an ambulance parked in front of the church, next to a police car. Several cops and medics stood at the entrance. I went to the side door and opened it. Priests gathered on the altar, each holding an aspergillum, the instrument used to sprinkle holy water on the congregation. My classmate, Martin Nell, stood at the altar, held at the elbows by two janitors, his palms folded in prayer at his diaphragm. Then he leapt off the marble floor and into the air, his hands still in front of him. He almost flew above the priests, a breeze mussing up the part in his hair which had been clean and straight. The janitors wrestled him back to the altar. He looked as if he were about to fly again when a priest came up behind me and took me outside by the arm. He said that the doors should have been locked, that they were performing an exorcism. He said I could never mention it to anyone, but if I had a regular confessor, I could tell him.

After that, I kept on eye on Nell. There were sixty of us in that third grade class, so something was always stirring—like fights in the cloak room, chalk throwing, farting contests. Every morning, Sister Mary Helene made us sit on half the seat of our desk. We had to leave the other half for our guardian angel, and sing:

Angel of God, my Guardian Dear,
To Whom God's love commits me here,
Ever this day be at my side
To light and guard, to rule and guide, amen.

Nell kept the entire seat. Sister approached him and he told her his angel was on his lap. She slapped him across the face, and when she did, she recoiled, holding her cheek, as if she had been slapped herself. She gave him a bewildered look, hiked her habit up with one hand and retreated to her desk.

Nell intrigued and repelled me. I talked with him now and then, but his presence made me dizzy, a feeling I enjoyed despite the queasiness. I was next to him one lunch period in the park across from the school. The principal, Sister Rose Aquinas, had instituted a "freeze bell" to signal the end of lunch time—we had to freeze in place—everyone had to stop playing tag, flipping baseball cards, or wrestling—when she rang the bell. She rang it a second time to release us from our frozen states to line up in an orderly way with our classes. I was about to put a piece of gum in my mouth when the bell rang. I froze, and so did Nell who was blowing soap bubbles from a plastic wand. The transparent sphere left the wand and then froze in front of his face. It hovered there, slightly shaking. Then the bell rang again and the bubble lifted. I had the dizzy feeling again which was becoming addictive.

That afternoon it snowed several inches and, at the end of the day, I followed Nell and his friends out the door, trailing a few steps behind them. He left no footprints. One of his friends mentioned this and Nell said that was because he was not walking on the snow, but on the "surface tension" of the snow. We all tried it without success. He seemed embarrassed and then sunk down like the rest of us, leaving tracks.

At Christmas, we had to give each other gifts, each boy assigned to another by lottery, and I drew Nell as my partner. The wrapped presents were to be opened at home, to avoid jealousies. My parents had taken me to the Merry-Go-Round toy store and I picked out what I wanted for myself: a Bulldog Tank that could climb over obstacles. I handed it to Martin and he gave me a box of equal heft. On Christmas morning, I opened it and was thrilled—a Steve Canyon Crash Helmet, complete with dark pilot goggles and a voice-changing oxygen mask. I loved it so much I only wore it indoors.

Our neighbors, the Humenicks, got a new refrigerator on Christmas week. A new refrigerator was big news on our block, not for the item, but for the box. We took turns standing in it, surrounded by four others, one on each side who pushed it and caught it, tipping and righting it, our homemade carnival ride. During my turn, an older boy, Richie Lamaga, who already shaved at thirteen, took over a side of the box. He shoved it toward Santo de Philippi, a tiny guy who could not stop it. It knocked him down and sent me shooting out head first into the bumper of a Ford. I pretended to be okay, but vomited in the middle of the night. My mother was concerned and tried to distract me by taking out her fortune telling deck, something I loved. The cards were faded and blurry and hard to decipher even by the light of day while in perfect health. The peacock, the ocean liner, the vase with a teardrop above it—I saw them all double and vomited again. I spent the next five nights in Elmhurst General Hospital for a concussion. Martin Nell came to see me, and asked why I wasn't wearing the helmet, that he had given it to me because he saw the accident coming. I was too shocked to question him further.

The last time I saw him was the following summer, at the Aquacade, a public swimming pool. He was betting kids that he could jump into the deepest part, sink to the bottom and walk to the shallow end. And he did. He couldn't float. The pool drew kids from all over Queens, so he always had new pigeons. Everyone paid up, happily, it was so weird. And after collecting the money, he did it once more, for free.

Oh, come on, John!

Charlie's father said to a midget on the corner, "Hey stretch, how's the weather down there?"

My alma mater, Fairfield University, offers a Master of Fine Arts in Creative Writing. Its mission statement reads, in part:

> It was conceptualized and executed to support, sustain, and extend the Jesuit ideal of developing the whole person. Writers, by their very nature, exemplify the principles of Ignatius: a search for self-knowledge, a pursuit of spiritual truth, a quest for intellectual knowledge, and a flowering of creative expression.
>
> Fairfield's program makes the connection between Jesuit philosophy and the graduate study of

> *creative writing even more pronounced and "syner-*
> *gistic," a word that in its Christian context suggests*
> *the pairing of the human and the divine for greater*
> *spiritual regeneration.*

Words can be stolen, but poetry can't be stolen.

Mr. DeTucci's reference letter written on my behalf to Fairfield University said I was full of vim and vigor. I wasn't sure what vim meant, so I looked it up. It said vigor. I looked up vigor and it said vim.

HYANNIS, MA — A restaurant with a Kennedy theme that opened late last month has already recast its cocktail menu to focus more on Camelot and less on controversy.

The Compound Bar and Grille, which opened May 24 at 644 Main St., less than four miles from the actual Kennedy compound in Hyannisport, features photos of JFK on the walls and the Kennedy name on some menu items.

Part of the theme, though, was eyebrow-raising: The restaurant's initial drinks menu listed cocktails with names such as the Honey Fitz and PT-109, but also included Dealey Plaza.

Dealey Plaza is the location in Dallas where President Kennedy was assassinated.

The drink is a mix of Smirnoff sorbet raspberry passion fruit and prosecco with raspberry-flavored ice.

New menus are expected today.

Gone are Dealey Plaza, Pink Chanel Suit (the suit Jackie Kennedy was wearing when her husband was shot) and Operation Aphrodite (the name of the World

War II operation in which Lt. Joseph P. Kennedy, Jr., was killed).

The drinks have been renamed Cool as a Cucumber, the U.S.S. Rose and the St. Crispin.

The artist who tries to paint a beautiful painting will fail. Beauty sought will never be captured. Beauty is a by-product of a full engagement with a subject.

In the early seventies, Meridian books published the Ethnic Prejudice in America Series, which included the titles, *Kike!—Anti-Semitism in America; Chink!—Anti-Chinese Prejudice in America; Mick!—Anti-Irish Prejudice in America, and Wop!—Anti-Italian Prejudice in America.*

A Dictionary of International Slurs (Ethnolphaulisms), by A. A. Roback is a systematic survey of name-calling among nations. Between the nasty slur and the aspiring slogan, Roback draws but one strong thread, the persistence of anti-Semitism. He lists slur expressions and derogatory proverbs, about 3,000 in all; these are organized sometimes according to the language source and to the group criticized, and sometimes merely alphabetically. His sources are twelve English compilations of slang and cant, eighty-two foreign dictionaries and thirty books cataloguing the proverbs of nations and folks. The proverbs are generally a safer source than slurs, since contexts and usage are less ambiguous, and, as witticisms, they may represent a more consolidated antagonism and argument.

The following transcript is a complete fabrication, written by the author and posted on his website. The author has admitted he was never on the show. A spokeswoman for Harpo, the entertainment company owned by Oprah Winfrey, said, "He has no relationship with Oprah's Book Club."

Oprah: The latest author to join my Book Club is a friend of mine who has just released his third novel, *Lost Tomorrow*, based on a true story about two young men who met in 1976 during America's Bicentennial. It was a time when our country was in turmoil. Disco and punk battled for radio airplay as our nation recovered from the Vietnam War. Coupled with the sexual revolution and divisive nature of the Watergate scandal, the rest of the world thought America was out of control.

Cut to Image of *Lost Tomorrow*'s Book Cover

Oprah: In direct contrast to the turmoil surrounding our country, Will—a flight attendant from southern California—and Adam—a medical student from Memphis, Tennessee, met and fell in love.

Return to Set

Oprah: *Lost Tomorrow* is a roller coaster journey through these two men's unique lives. So fasten your seat belts because you are about to meet the author of *Lost Tomorrow*, who flew in from Cape Cod, Massachusetts, just to spend some time with us today.

Oprah: I must tell you that I immediately fell in love with this book when I first read it.

Author: Thank you. Thanks very much.

Oprah: *Lost Tomorrow* is truly a gem of story. Tell me how you came to write this very poignant book.

Author: Well, Oprah, it's a story that really tugged at my heartstrings and, ah, I felt very certain about this being a story that needed to be shared...

"After three days of that cure, he died..."

He was a bold man that first eat an oyster.

When a dog sees his master leave the house, he wonders if he'll ever return. When man saw the sun set for the first time, he must have wondered if it would ever rise again.

B. J. Lifton, when told of the death of her close friend, said, "How unlike Helen."

The best-selling, middle-aged novelist eventually married the young hostess at the local restaurant. A few months after the wedding, I walked past their house and saw him reading in an overstuffed armchair, a heavy book in his lap. The bride stood at the window, looking out at the street, both palms against the glass.

"Younger Girl" was a big hit for The Critters.

At twenty-four, Baudelaire tried to commit suicide. The note he wrote said that the effort of falling asleep and the effort of waking had become unbearable to him.

Coffee in the morning to arouse consciousness. Gin in the evening to obliterate what you became conscious of during the day.

> The woods are lovely, dark and deep…
> from "Stopping by Woods on a Snowy
>   Evening" by Robert Frost (1922)

> Our bed is lovely, dark, and sweet…
> from "The Phantom Wooer"
>   by Thomas Lovell Beddoes (1849)

Well, we are officially desperate. My folks have been unable to sell their house in Florida. The market is really flat and, even though it is listed with Century 21, nothing has come of it. So: This mass email to everyone I could think of to ask for your help and/or advice. If you know of anyone (age 55 or over!) who is even remotely interested in buying a home in Florida, please have them contact me. Also, if you could pass on this plea to folks in your email address book and ask them to pass it on (sort of like a real estate chain letter!) that would be terrific. Let me know, also, of any advertising opportunities that would be good to use. I shall include a description of the property for you—

Joe and Barb's house in Florida: FOR SALE: two bedroom, two bath permanent mobile home in a 55+ retirement park in Clearwater, FL, five minutes from Tampa. The appliances are old, but they work, and furniture, including a washer and dryer, is included in the selling price ($70,000—reduced from $85,000, but still negotiable). There is no yard, really, but there is a carport and washer and dryer hookup in the outdoor storage shed. My folks will throw in the chickens too—I'm joking! It is right off Route 19, near shopping areas and about five miles from the beach, but it is NOT in a flood plain and has never sustained any damage during any of the significant hurricanes/tropical storms of years past. The Ranch Mobile Home Park has a pool, a clubhouse, a Homeowners' Association that sponsors various activities (I personally have attended a New Year's Dance and a July 4ᵗʰ Cookout there and can attest to the fact that they are rocking times!), and a rather conscientious security patrol (who, when we were visiting once, stopped my teenage son Andrew, who was walking around by himself, looking suspicious, I guess, and asked him what he was doing there!). People watch out for each other, and my parents certainly enjoyed living there over the past 25 years. For someone looking to move to Florida permanently or for anyone interested in having a place to spend the winter (it is completely furnished—you could move in right now), it would be perfect.

One millennium at a time.

Frank Sinatra's checklist for what he wanted in a woman:
1.   Beautiful
2.   Classy
3.   Pedigreed
4.   Intelligent
5.   Big Eyes
6.   Thin
7.   Sleek Legs
8.   Irish Catholic
9.   Natural (minimal makeup and perfume)
10. Healthy (doesn't smoke)
11. Immaculate
12. Blind Devotion

If you put your hand down a duck's throat, all the way through the body and out his rear end and then turn him inside out, he vanishes. That's the Zen Duck Pop.

When I was twenty, I fell in love with Claire, the most beautiful woman I'd met. She was my age, recently divorced and living alone in a house at the top of hill that overlooked the bay. We had mutual friends, and often ate dinner at their houses, and went out together for drinks in a group.

She never showed any interest in me, although I had made my affection plain in little hints, bits of quoted poems and sophomoric jokes I thought sly.

One late night at a bar, she stared into my eyes as if I were someone else and said, "Let's get our coats." When we arrived at the house on the hill, she couldn't find her keys. We were locked out.

She handed me a heavy snow shovel that had been leaning against the doorframe, and said to smash the glass, which I did, ramming the blade so it shattered the long window completely, crashing it to our feet in a long waterfall of shards, waking the houses below.

In my sixty-second year, I can still hear the glass falling.

Afternoon sunlight hit the globe in my little son's room, making Alaska as warm as Florida.

The only remedy is to break everything.

Casting off with Captain Crosby was like attending a church service. He addressed all the men as Mister. "You may cast off now, Mr. Sousa," he would remark quietly, and they would chug across the harbor which was only now filling with light. When a tuna tore his nets to pieces, he referred to "that ding-dong fish."

Her eyes would blink: "Now you see what I mean?
You mean to say that you haven't seen?"
    Jules Laforgue, 1886

It is impossible to say just what I mean!...
If one, settling a pillow or throwing off a shawl,
And turning toward the window, should say:
"That is not it at all,
That is not what I meant, at all."
    T. S. Eliot, 1915

And often—I can already hear myself now—
Say to the other, "Had I but known..."
But married, too, would each not on his own
Have also said, "Had I but known..."
    Laforgue

For I have known them all already, known them all—
Have known the evenings, mornings, afternoons,
I have measured out my life with coffee spoons...
    Eliot

Pick your spots, baby. Pick your spots.

Name a female sonneteer.
    Oh no! It's National Poetry Month!

The architect looked at the building and said, "It's like a beautiful woman with thick ankles."

The porcupine is the only vegetable in the animal kingdom.

In my memoir class there was a brilliant young woman in a wheelchair who spoke with great difficulty. She had had her neck manipulated by an incompetent chiropractor and the result was Locked-in Syndrome: a condition in which a patient is aware and awake but cannot move or communicate verbally due to complete paralysis of nearly all voluntary muscles in the body except for the eyes. Her favorite book was Elias Canetti's *The Tongue Set Free*.

I should not talk so much about myself if there were anybody else I knew as well.

Called a fraud for saying he had extra-terrestrial experiences, Richard Shaver kept repeating, "I only know that I remember Lemuria."

The summer dinner party was weird because one of the guests described herself as a moth-er, and brought moth-attracting lights. As cocktails were served, the hostess provided the requested sheets which the moth-er draped over privet hedges, illuminating them with the lights. Between courses, guests left the table and were stunned by the odd varieties covering the linens and named by the expert: Inconsolable Underwing, Flame Shouldered Dart and PawPaw Sphinx.

160
22

I realized that Allen Grossman had remained seated and went back to join him. We discussed Hart Crane and I said I found him a difficult poet. He said he was not difficult at all. A couple of artists returned and asked what we were talking about. I explained the subject and gave an example of why I found Crane difficult, quoting, "outspoken buttocks in pink beads" and "mustard scansions of the eyes." They were puzzled by the last phrase and said so.

Grossman said, "It's very simple, the scansions are the marks around the eyes, and they are the color of mustard, which is what you put on your hot *dog*."

The waitress recommended the roast turkey which she said was dressed with filling. I asked her what was in the filling. She said, "Filling."

Podunk, Gipip, Pennsyltucky and Bimbombey.

Clearing weeds from the garden beds, impressed how many of them mimic the flowers they grow alongside, I am not ridding the area of unsightliness, but of the drain they place on the lilies, the astilbe, the clematis, by stealing their water and soil nutrients. I can't help compare it to excising clichés that steal the thunder from a page of otherwise good writing.

I've been teaching too long.

In the middle of his lecture, the speaker at the conference asked the audience to rise to illustrate a point. Later, he was criticized for ignoring those not able to stand, and for rolling three kinds of micro-aggressions into one: *pathologizing, second class citizen* and *environmental.*

John Zacherle, host of television horror movies, came on the air accompanied by a voice screaming, "Let me out of here," dragging out that last syllable. He was extremely popular. It is everyman's cry.

As an only child, I was alone for days on end. I learned to love my toy soldiers, my men, and set them up in forts and castles. I heard my mother on the phone complimenting my self-sufficiency. I took this as a great accolade, and when guests arrived and asked what I was doing, I would announce that I could play "with myself for hours." My mother hopelessly tried to correct me. "*By* yourself!" she yelled. "*By* yourself!"

People usually die doing what they do most of the time. The Kennedy family and their love of leisure: they die skiing, flying a plane to Martha's Vineyard, exercising in a health club.

In my role as chair I heard a complaint from a female student that her professor held conferences at his apartment in Cambridge in a room unfurnished except for a couch. As he was her thesis director, he had to meet her often, and she felt uncomfortable.

I spoke with the teacher and he became indignant. He said that he conferred with many students at his place. I asked if he met any male students on this couch. The answer was none.

Lana never recovered from a bad acid trip and suffered from fierce migraines. She said that walking backward alleviated them. And so she walked backward for a year. Yes, for a whole year she walked backward down Commercial Street, through the aisles of the A&P. She even waited in line backwards at the Drop-In Center, got her prescription and walked backwards to have it filled at Adams Pharmacy. No one said anything, everyone acted as if it were perfectly normal. That's P'town. One night, some guys at the Fo'c's'le argued over whether or not she was faking it and after a few drinks two of them went to her house and peered into the windows. They came back and said it was for real, she was walking backward from room to room.

A neighbor's wife was leaving for a week, and her husband was worried about maintaining the house in her absence. His friend told him that an hour before she returned, he should dunk a rag in Murphy's Oil Soap and run it around the front door jamb, so the first scent she noticed would be that of cleanliness and industry.

Radio ads in the sixties were written in poetry for a men's clothing store in Union, New Jersey that was open nineteen hours a day from 10 A.M. 'til 5 A.M.:

> Dennison Joe's: Where Money Talks and Nobody
>   Walks.
> Dennison, the men's clothier, Route 22, Union, N.J.,
>   wants you to know
> there's a wise old owl sitting up in the tree who says
> there's nothing I see at day that interests me.

I buy at night, I buy right. Never buy at a store that
        closes at 4.
You'll try the door, you'll read the sign: we close
        at 4.
So you take the next day off and lose 75 bucks in pay.
Get back to the store that closes at 4.
Now you see a sign. Lunch: 12 to 1. You look at the
        time, it's 12:30.
And you blow your top. You try the door. Then the
        rain came, and did it pour.
Now you're wet and sore. Then he came and you're
        in the store.
So you bought a $75 suit and the $75 you lost in
        pay adds up to $150.
Now, Dennison says that for that kind of dough I
        will sell you three.
Fill our till that's nil.
That's Dennison Clothier, Route 22, Union,
        New Jersey.
Open from 10 A.M. until 5 the next morning.
Recognized charge plans accepted, and open
        right now.

I worked out with 15 pound dumbbells, then moved to
20. Then 25. Back to 20, 15. Now 8 pounders lay near
the liquor cabinet, covered in dust.

Art: the struggle between what we want to do and what
we are able to do. Like being very young or very old.

At Dennison's, several babes were there every night. They
were selling more than just clothes, but I didn't know it.

164
22

I've written every plot there is, but they all come down to one: things are not what they seem.

I euthanized my dog, Major, at the Queens Animal Hospital. I can still smell the scent of alcohol swabbed over the examining table. The vet injected his front paw as I circled him in my arms, feeling his back legs collapse, and then the front. I laid him down. I moved to scratch behind his ear and then stopped my hand mid-air, pointless. I had walked in with a dog and walked out with a leash.

To find the mandrake, one needs the black dog.

Literature was born not the day when a boy crying *wolf wolf* came running out of the Neanderthal valley with a big gray wolf at his heels: literature was born on the day when a boy came crying *wolf wolf* and there was no wolf behind him. That the poor little fellow was finally eaten up by a real beast because he lied too often is quite incidental. But here is what is important. Between the wolf in the tall grass and the wolf in the tall story there is a shimmering go-between. That go-between, that prism, is the art of literature.

At a lunch break at our three-day academic retreat, the eldest, most distinguished and most staid member of the Performing Arts department came up to me and pointed to the lone undergraduate representative, Charlotte. Blonde, pale and beautiful, Charlotte and her English accent transfixed the room. My colleague said, "John, I love my Miriam, but when I look over at

Charlotte during this three-day stretch of boredom, I have such thoughts that I cry, 'Lord have mercy on my soul!' "

Mark Rothko, standing in front of the Rembrandt self-portrait at the Frick, said, "What a great Jewish actor Rembrandt was, as if a tear could come from the corner of an eye at any moment."

Cheever: Part of the thrill of being told a story is the chance of being hoodwinked or taken. The telling of lies is a sort of sleight of hand that displays our deepest feelings about life.

Interviewer: Can you give an example of a preposterous lie that tells a great deal about life?

Cheever: Indeed. The vows of Holy Matrimony.

Ninety percent of the people in the world end up with the wrong person. And that's what makes the jukebox spin.

Sister Grace called on me to read from *Fun with Dick and Jane* in front of the class for Principal Sister Rose Aquinas. I froze at the second sentence. The principal sent me to the dunce chair where I sat with my back to the class, and she left in a huff, disappointed in the class because of me. Sister Grace told me to get back to my seat, saying, "You're my little soldier and you will fight another day."

I fought only to lose all the other days, horrified of public speaking. A year later, my mother tried to get me to regain my confidence by enrolling me in a class taught by the Toastmasters, where the instructor said to imagine each member of the audience totally nude. I did, and I vomited.

Don't dig your fox-hole so deep you can't see over the top.

Time cures all ills. But time causes all ills.

> All night long
> We would sing that stupid song
> And every word we sang
> I knew was true
> Are you with me, Doctor Wu?

I return to my childhood home on Judge Street in Elmhurst for my twenty-first birthday party. My mother looks out the second story window and points to a boy sitting in a tree eye-level with her. She says, "This boy is peeping on us and telling all of our secrets."

We go into the yard, and I tell my mother I have a cut on my wrist that won't heal.

She examines it and says it's infected.

She squeezes my wrist, and blood flows out, followed by a worm. She continues to squeeze and worm after worm appears, each falling into the garden. When twenty-one worms emerge, the cut closes.

A tenor who collapsed and died on stage at the Metropolitan Opera House just after singing, "You can only live so long," had no previous heart condition or medical problems, his manager said. Richard Versalle, 63, who was alone on stage, had just sung the line in the opening scene of *The Makropulos Case*, a 1926 Czech opera, on Friday night, when he fell from a ladder.

Once you have kissed a corpse on the forehead there always remains something on your lips, a distant bitterness, an aftertaste of the void that nothing will efface.

"When the sun rises, do you not see a round disc of fire somewhat like a guinea?"

"O no, no, I see an innumerable company of the heavenly host crying, 'Holy, Holy, Holy is the Lord God Almighty.'"

Music is the greatest means we have of digesting time.

My earliest memory is dipped in red. I come out of a door on the arm of a maid, the floor in front of me is red, and to the left a staircase goes down, equally red. Across from us, at the same height, a door opens, and a smiling man steps forth, walking towards me in a friendly way. He steps close to me, halts, and says, "Show me your tongue." I stick out my tongue, he reaches into his pocket, pulls out a jackknife, opens it, and brings the blade all the way to my tongue. He says, "Now we'll cut off his tongue." I don't dare pull back my tongue. He comes closer and closer, the blade will touch me any second. In the last moment, he pulls back the knife, saying, "Not today, tomorrow." He snaps the knife shut again and puts it back in his pocket.

Years later I realized that this was my babysitter's lover, frightening me into silence about their rendezvous. The threat with the knife worked, the child literally held his tongue for ten years.

He talked not to explain himself, but to conceal himself.

Hello, Walls.

Vaudeville performer Eva Tanguay, aka, the Cyclonic One, sang her original songs,
"It's All Been Done Before But Not the Way I Do It," and "That's Why They Call Me Tabasco," while wearing a dress of pennies which she plucked off and threw to the audience, a feat her biographer says marked the first time a stripper tipped the crowd and not vice versa.

Once the limo has reached its destination, nothing prevents the chauffeur from being shot.

Torschlusspanik. "Gate-closing panic." The fear of ever-diminishing opportunities as one grows old.

I remember you. The guy with the glasses. You used to sit in the window of the Old Colony. Yeah, the guy with the glasses! Can you see any better now?

> They never re-opened that worthless pit,
> they just placed a marble stand in front of it.

Four walls. Four walls. No matter how many times they add themselves up, they always come out four.

Until a few decades ago, you did not exist. In a few more decades, you will once again not exist. From the beginning of time, until the end of time, non-existence is your natural state. So life is a brief interruption to your natural state of non-existence.

A life has a beginning, a middle and an end, but not necessarily in that order.

In with a dog, out with a leash.

quale [kwä-lay]: *Eng.* n 1. A property (such as hardness) considered apart from things that have that property. 2. A property that is experienced as distinct from any source it may have in a physical object. *Ital.* pron.a. 1. Which, what. 2. Who. 3. Some. 4. As, just as.